THE UNBREAKABLE STALLION — MOONSHINE !

As though a voice from behind bade him turn, he swung sharply and saw what seemed a cloud of moonlight gathered into a moving form, half shadow, half mist, half brilliance. It glided over a hilltop, disappeared in the wash of shade that filled a gully, and slipped into view again over a closer rise of ground. It was Moonshine.

He neighed a challenge, or a gloating over the dead man, then whirled and fled. Oh, the swing and lightness of that stride—like a wave in the free ocean.

It was hard to turn back, for a power drew him down the trail of the horse. Between his knees he could sense the lithe, strong barrel of Moonshine, and his face was hot with longing to feel the wind of Moonshine's galloping.

He found himself in the dugout with his head between his hands. When he sprang up his mind was clear.

This note he scrawled: "I GOT A HURRY CALL, AND I AM GONE."

Books by Max Brand

Ambush at Torture Canyon
The Bandit of the Black Hills
The Bells of San Filipo
Black Jack
Blood on the Trail
The Blue Jay
The Border Kid
Danger Trail
Dead or Alive
Destry Rides Again
The False Rider
Fightin' Fool
Fightin' Four
Flaming Irons
Galloping Danger
Ghost Rider (Original title: Clung)
The Gun Tamer
Gunman's Reckoning
Harrigan
Hired Guns
Hunted Riders
The Jackson Trail
Larromee's Ranch
The Longhorn Feud
The Longhorn's Ranch
The Long, Long Trail
The Man from Mustang
The Night Horseman
On the Trail of Four

The Outlaw
The Outlaw of Buffalo Flat
The Phantom Spy
Pillar Mountain
Pleasant Jim
The Reward
Ride the Wild Trail
Riders of the Plains
Rippon Rides Double
Rustlers of Beacon Creek
The Seven of Diamonds
Seven Trails
Shotgun Law
Silvertip's Search
Silvertip's Trap
Singing Guns
Single Jack
Steve Train's Ordeal
The Stingaree
The Stolen Stallion
The Streak
The Tenderfoot
Thunder Moon
Tragedy Trail
Trouble Kid
The Untamed
Valley of the Vanishing Men
Valley Thieves
Vengeance Trail

Published by POCKET BOOKS

Max Brand

GALLOPING DANGER

PUBLISHED BY POCKET BOOKS NEW YORK

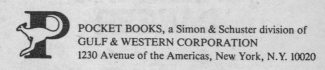

POCKET BOOKS, a Simon & Schuster division of
GULF & WESTERN CORPORATION
1230 Avenue of the Americas, New York, N.Y. 10020

ISBN: 0-671-41514-X

First Pocket Books printing January, 1981

10 9 8 7 6 5 4 3 2 1

POCKET and colophon are trademarks of Simon & Schuster.

Printed in the U.S.A.

GALLOPING
DANGER

1

ECONOMY, whether of money or of labor, was carried by Mrs. E. Garrison to the nth degree, for economy of all kinds was necessary to the maintenance of her family. She had eight sons and no daughters. Three of the sons had been born at one time, and two at another. She threw herself with devotion into the battle to support these eight lives decently. A remnant of youth and good looks she sacrificed first, then all her time, her temper, her powers of body and soul went into the endless struggle, and she was so far victorious that neither Mrs. Oldham, right-hand neighbor, nor Mrs. Taylor on her left could ever find spot or speck on the new-burnished faces of the Garrison boys when they herded off to school in the morning. Work turned her to a famine-stricken wraith. But her heart grew stronger as she saw the fruit of her agony, eight boys with straight bodies and fresh, clear eyes.

On this wash-Monday, having hung out the sheets and the pillowcases, the napkins, and the tablecloths, and all the "whites," she dragged the clothesbasket back to the kitchen to start the colored articles boiling in the same water which had served for the first batch. Time was when she had changed the water for each set of clothes, but now that her shoulders cracked under the weight of the boiler she moved it as seldom as possible.

"Besides," as she said, "clear water ain't what cleans 'em; it's the boiling and the soap and the blessed elbow-grease."

Yet, on this day, having dumped the colored things into the boiler and opened the door of the stove to shovel in more coal, she discovered that the last live cinder was turning from red to black; the fire was out! It was a calamity, for already the afternoon wore on, and she must rush to finish the washing in time to cook supper; that was the only point on which her husband was adamant—meals had to be punctual. Then she thought of assistance, and remembered that her eldest son was home; the teacher of his class was ill, which accounted for the vacation.

"The great lummox!" muttered Mrs. Garrison. "He ought to have been down here hours ago, helpin' me hang out and rinsin'." She went to the foot of the back stairs, narrow, unpainted, and dark, the one untidy place of the house.

"Oh, Lee!" she called. "Lee!"

From above, half whine, half growl: "Yes?"

"Come down here this minute and chop me some kindling. The fire's out."

"Wait till I finish this page."

"I'll wait for nothing. You come hopping, young man."

She heard the clap of the book being shut, the sound of heavy footfalls overhead, and she went into the dining room for an instant's rest. It was a hot day in June, with just enough breeze to drag the smoke from the factories over the town, filling the air with a thick, sweet odor of soot. Mrs. Garrison relaxed in her husband's armchair in the coolest

8

corner of the room and bent her head to think over the dishes for supper. She closed her eyes, too, and in a moment she was asleep, but she kept on working in her dream, heard the kindling dumped with a rattle on the kitchen floor, and dragged herself from the chair to open the dampers so that the fire roared and the water began to foam in the boiler.

In reality, Lee Garrison had not left his room. That noisy closing of the book, the thumping of his feet on the floor, were all a ruse. He had only sat forward in his chair and drummed with his heels; his thumb kept the place when he snapped the book shut, and now he opened it, still sitting on the edge of the chair, still bending to rise, while his eye swept through the rest of the adventure. For ten swarthy giants had just started into the path of Lancelot and barred his way to the perilous chapel with a voice of thunder. They scattered again as the good knight put forward his shield and drew his sword against such great odds as these, and Lee Garrison went with Lancelot into the chapel itself, where only one light burned and where the corpse lay "hylled in silk."

He did not change that cramped position, as if about to rise. It was hours later when he heard the deep voice of his father downstairs, and his mother pouring out a protest; then he laid aside his "Malory" with a sigh and stood up. Plainly he would never approach the height or the bulk of William Garrison, but he gave promise of the same broad shoulders, together with better proportions and, throughout, a fine workmanship of which there was little trace in either his father or mother. He was their first-born, and sometimes his mother thought, inarticulately, that the bloom of their youth, their first great joy, their hopes and their dreams, had all gone into the body and soul of Lee. The eyes of the seven were straight and clear with good health, but the eyes of Lee held both a black shadow and a light which were his alone. Even when he was a tiny fellow he seemed to be thinking more than he spoke, and she had an odd feeling that he often judged her; therefore she both dreaded and loved him. He was not demonstrative, otherwise his father would have idolized him. For the rest, he was the laziest boy in Waybury, rumor said. Books had been his world for five years, now, but though his father and his mother often lectured him about this all-consuming passion, they secretly respected it and hoped for great things.

He turned over his situation calmly, for he had swept through so many crises in books that he had little enthusiasm left for the troubles of real life. His mother was accusing him bitterly. It would have meant a hard thrashing if any of the other boys had been the culprit, but his father had always had a strange aversion for caning Lee, and now the worst he could expect would be imprisonment in a dark room without supper. That was the usual punishment, for he wisely never had let them know that it was almost as pleasant to dream in the dark as to read in the light.

"Lee!" called his father. On the way downstairs he heard his mother reiterate: "I just told him to chop some kindling. Then I sat down for a minute and somehow, I don't know just how it happened, but—"

"That'll do, Mother. The point is, supper ain't ready, and Lee's to blame. I got to eat if I'm goin' to work, don't I?"

"Hush up, William. Do hush up, or Lucy Ganning'll hear, and it'll be over the neighborhood in a jiffy." Lucy Ganning was a shrewd-eyed spinster living across the street.

"Darn Lucy Ganning!" cried the father. "Come here, Lee!"

The kitchen was in deep shadow, and to Lee, coming down the stairs, it seemed as if his father towered to the ceiling. The soot of the forge was furrowed by perspiration;

it was an ugly mask, rather than a face, the eyes looking out through holes rimmed with white. His father's great black hand crushed Lee's shoulder and lifted him from the floor.

"Now," said William Garrison, fighting to control himself, "tell me the straight of this."

"He slapped his book shut and made as if he was coming down," cried the mother. "I went and sat down—"

Lee hunted swiftly for a convincing lie, found none, and told the truth.

"I just stopped to finish the page, Dad, honest. And then a minute later you came home."

His mother laughed hysterically. "Will you listen to that? Look at the stove. It's cold, ain't it? It's been two hours long, that minute of Lee's."

"D'you think I'd lie? Dad, it wasn't hardly more'n a minute."

"Lee, how d'you dare say such things? And there he sat all day upstairs never offering to help me, while I was breaking my back with that boiler, and—" Her voice shook; she was mute with self-pity and rage.

"So that's what you been doin'?" said William Garrison. Lee looked sharply at his father and for the first time in his life was really afraid; the big man spoke quietly, but he spoke through his teeth, and he seemed a stranger. Through the dining-room door Lee saw seven white faces; little Jerry and Peter, the twins, were clasping each other in terror.

"You been up there with your books! Your mother was down here slaving. I was up to the forge with fire in my face!"

They were silent, looking at each other, until Lee saw that his father was trembling.

"William," whispered the mother, "William, what d'you aim to do?"

"Close that door!"

She stared at him a moment and then went silently and shut the door across the seven white faces. She came back and reached out her hand, but she did not touch her husband with it.

"William!" she whispered again.

"I'm going to teach him."

She fumbled and caught the back of a chair.

"Don't look that way, Mother," broke out Lee. "I'm not afraid."

"Hush!" she cried, but William Garrison had balled both his great fists.

"You don't fear me, eh?" he said, grinding out the words. "Well, by heaven, you will fear me. D'you hear that? My own son don't fear me!" The big hands clamped on Lee's shoulders and wrenched him about. "Listen to me. I been lettin' you go your own sweet way. That's ended. You're no good, and you're comin' to no good end. I'm goin' to make you or break you, and I'm goin' to do it now."

There was no doubt about it. It meant a thrashing, and Lee wondered if he would scream as the others screamed. The thought made him sick. He wanted to die before the test came.

"William," said his mother in that same terrifying whisper, "it wasn't much he done wrong." The big man only turned his head and looked at her, and his fingers worked deeper into the shoulders of Lee. "I'll get the switch," she said.

"Switch? Switch nothing!"

She was upon him with a cry, her hands clutching at the breast of her husband.

"William, you ain't goin' to touch him? You ain't in the right way for it. You—you'll kill him. My baby!"

"Molly, you go sit down."

She wavered, and then dropped into a chair and hugged her face in her arms.

"Don't do it, Dad," said Lee. "Don't you see? She can't stand it."

His father blinked as though a fierce light had been flashed in his face.

"Good heaven!" groaned William Garrison. "A coward, too!"

By one hand he still held Lee, and now he turned and strode out of the kitchen and down the back steps, dragging the boy. He threw back the cellar doors with a crash and went down with Lee carried in front by the scruff of the neck. Below it was almost night, and now that the dimness covered the face of his father, Lee, standing in the corner, felt the horror slip from him. He remembered that worried, gentle face which had leaned above him when he had had scarlet fever.

"Dad," he said, "I'm not afraid, but wait till tomorrow. It's worse on Mother than it is on me."

"The devil!" said William Garrison hoarsely, and he caught up a billet of wood from the floor. That voice told Lee plainly that he had to do with a stranger, an enemy. He looked about him, and in the corner stood the wooden sword which he had whittled out when he first read the story of "Excalibur." He caught it by the flimsy hilt.

"I give you warning," he said in a high, small voice, "I'm going to fight back."

"You are, eh? Come here!"

Out of the dark a hand reached at him, and he struck it away with the wooden sword. That first blow was the last; Excalibur snapped at the flimsy hilt. A great black form rushed on him. He was whirled about. A bruising, cutting blow whacked on his shoulders. Lee could have wept with

13

joy, for the pain, instead of leaping out at his teeth in a shriek, traveled inward, a deep, silent hurt. There was only the sound of the blows, the harsh breathing of his father, the staggering impacts, and shooting, burning pains.

A pause with lifted hand. "Have you got enough?" gasped out William Garrison, and a great sense of unfairness rushed through Lee and made tears come in his eyes. He was not being punished; he was being fought as a grown man fights an equal, and all his sense of fair play revolted. If he could have spoken he would have defied the giant in the dark, but he dared not open his lips for fear of the sobs which made his throat ache.

"Have you got enough?" repeated William Garrison, thundering. Then: "I guess that'll do you for a while." He seemed to grow sober at a stride. "Son, I thought you was a coward; maybe I was wrong. You stay here and think it over—what you done and how you lied; I'm coming back later on."

Mr. Garrison disappeared up the steps, the cellar doors crashed shut, and the padlock snapped. At that Lee forgot his pain.

"He wouldn't trust me!" he whispered to himself. "He wouldn't trust me. He locked me up like a dog that's been whipped!"

Lee shook his fist in a silent fury of shame and hate and then sat down to think. Vital, deep emotions did not last long in Lee. His edge had been taken by romance, his sensibilities blunted, but as he heard the noise of supper preparations begin over his head, he was sure of one thing; he would not face his seven brothers in the morning and see their half-sheepish, half-mocking grins. He was like them, now; something to be beaten into obedience. Then there was a deep rumbling—his father's laugh!

He could not believe it, for a time. Then silverware jingled faintly. They sat at the table; they had forgotten.

"And I'll forget you!" said Lee in a burst of sorrow and choking shame. "I'll forget you all, forever!"

It was a simple matter to escape through the cellar window, which, of course, his father had forgotten, and it was equally easy to steal across the kitchen floor while Paul was telling a noisy anecdote about the school. His voice covered the sound of Lee's steps, but through the dining-room door Lee saw his mother's sad face, and he blessed her for it.

Once in the room which he shared with three of his brothers, he lighted the oil lamp and swiftly set about making up his bundle. In five minutes he was on his way downstairs.

He stopped at the foot of them to listen. If there had been one word for him, one syllable to show they missed him, he would have turned back, but they were all exclaiming about something he did not understand, and Lee went out into the night.

2

THERE are some who alter little between youth and manhood, and Lee Garrison was one of these. He was thirteen when he curled up in the corner of a freight car and awoke a little later with the wheels jolting beneath him. A dozen years later, if any one from Wayburg had come across a certain tanned line rider in the Llano Estacado, he would probably have recognized Lee in spite of sombrero and chaps. His shoulders had broadened to the full of their early promise. His face was little changed. At thirteen he had looked much older than his age; at twenty-five he seemed much younger.

Most cattlemen have to hold themselves to the monotony of their work by steady effort, consciously tensed to be prepared for little things, straining their eyes across miles of shimmering sand to watch the herds and mark the sick or the strayed, until the crowfoot wrinkles come, the brows draw down; and boys acquire a grim, wistful expression that should not be theirs until middle age. But Lee Garrison was not one of those who fight nature; he accepted it. His nearest approach to the alert was quiet watchfulness like that of the dog which sees the rabbit but prefers hunger to the long race in the heat. No doubt this accounted for Lee's unwrinkled forehead. From a distance he appeared calmly dignified; at close hand his face was rather a blank, except for the occasional swift play of his eyes, and the southwest, which has not time to ponder over idiosyncrasies or exceptions, put down Lee Garrison as a lazy man and filed him away in its memory under that heading.

Even granting the celebrated vacuity of Lee's mind, men wondered how he could stick to line riding. Hour by hour, day by day, week by week, month by month, he journeyed up and down a hundred miles of fence, never visited except by the chuck wagon, and traveling to the ranch house, fifteen miles away, only on state occasions. Even at round-up time, when he could have made his five dollars and head as a bronc-peeler, he chose rather to keep up that deadly routine which drives more sensitive cow-punchers mad. Always he was loading down the fence with that infinite line of posts fogging into view, dipping now and again into a hollow, or swaying in or out to avoid a rock, but usually only a line which went straight across a flat earth, a string of heads dwindling and bobbing up and down to the trot of his horse.

Twelve hours a day he kept the saddle with hammer, nails, pliers, wire stretcher, and boot sack full of staples. The posts were old, the staples worked loose, and it was a continual mounting and dismounting, a blow with the hammer, a staple sent home, and then back into the saddle again, only to see a strand sagging a dozen yards ahead. Off again, on again, all day, every day—the patience of Indians themselves often gave way to gibbering idiocy after a few months of this labor, but Lee Garrison held out; he stayed by preference. One might have thought that he loved the quiet and nature as the old trout fisher loves it—but the staked plains! Countless Spanish daggers were all that showed above ground level. There were not mountains rolling against the horizon, cool and blue. For life, therefore, the prairie dogs!

It was one of those which made Lee pause in the very act of lifting his horse into a canter to head for the nearest of his dugouts; for it would be dark by the time he had finished his supper and haste was needed, but the prairie dog stood by his mound looking like a miniature beaver, his tail "jiggering" up and down with the fury of his barking. A companion jumped out of the hole and joined in the defiance.

"Sassy little devil," murmured Garrison, and jerked out his revolver. The bullet merely knocked a spray of sand over the prairie dogs as they whirled toward safety.

It was a result which Lee had small time to observe, for his horse leaped straight into the air and came down stiff-legged, swallowing his head. Past five posts he bucked with educated viciousness, but at the sixth he tossed up his head and looked back at the rider as though asking pardon for such folly; even a painful jab of the spurs only made him switch his tail and break into a perfectly measured lope. The face of the rider, which had lighted for an instant, now went blank again.

"Of all the no-good hosses I ever see," said the master, "you're the worst and the yaller-heartedest, Pinto. When you come out to me I had hopes of you."

The pinto cocked a wary ear back and turned the corner of a red-stained eye.

"But," concluded the line rider, "now you can't pitch enough to make conversation."

Yes, he undoubtedly could ride as well as the next man, but as a marksman he was distinctly ordinary. But the sigh he heaved was not on account of the missed shot; it was what that miss signified. When he first arrived in the cattle country his boy mind had been filled with a glamour of it, and he had begun to school himself to be a model knight of the plains—expert rider, shot, and cattleman, knowing all the desert and the creatures of the desert. Only in one ambition had he succeeded; he could stick in a saddle as though he were glued to the leather, but all his other aspirations were so long dead that the thought of them barely served to awaken in him a faint melancholy regret.

At the dugout he unsaddled his horse and hobbled him carefully, for Pinto's chief talent and ambition was to break and run for the ranch house fifteen miles away.

Next he prepared his supper from the food cached in the dugout, and within an hour after his arrival he had cooked and eaten his supper and spread his bed.

It was a gray, cold evening, more like January than March, and the high mist which was hardly noticeable during the day now shut away the color of the sunset and the sun went down red. The prairie dogs no longer chattered, but a bull bat sat on the nearest fence post wailing at him like a whippoorwill, and twice a prairie-dog owl, hunting close to the ground, skimmed past the dugout, a living shadow, uttering the sad cry which always seems to come from a great distance.

So Lee Garrison made himself comfortable in the dugout, lounging with a saddle for a pillow, and a clean lantern ready behind his head, though it was not yet dark enough for artificial light. Behind him lay three books, which he touched after the manner of the after-dinner smoker, fingering his cigars and considering which flavor he will choose. It was some time before he made up his mind, and indeed, to a lover of this sort of reading there was little measure of preference among three such fountainheads of romance as the "Arabian Nights," "Boccaccio," and "Malory." These were his treasury, of which he never wearied, each of them exhaustless in incident, thronging with pictures.

But he suited his daily selection to his mood, having sometimes a taste for the voluptuous adventures of the Arabian tales; or often for "Boccaccio," wicked, delightful, chuckling at sin and even smiling at virtue; but most frequently, as on this evening, he chose the *Morte d' Arthur*. It was his first love among books and would remain his last, for though the "Arabian Nights" might cloy, or "Boccaccio" grow tiresome, he never lost his passion for those whom "Malory" keeps alive in sword and armor at Whitsuntide in Camelot, or at the gate of some dark castle in the forest.

Again on this night it was "Malory." The ragged covers opened, the pages, chipped at the corners, yellowed, stained, slipped away of their own accord; and in ten seconds he saw the knight with the covered shield send Tristram hurtling out of his saddle—a mighty fall! And he rolled thrice over, grasping his hands full of dirt each time. Lee Garrison followed the fight with motions of his clenched right hand.

Such was his absorption that he heard neither the rattling approach of the chuck wagon nor the long haloo of the driver. Not until Baldy stood at the door, filling it, and his shadow fell across the book, did Lee look up.

"What I'd like to know," shouted Baldy, without other greeting, "is why the devil you don't have regular stopping places regular times. I started this morning right after chow, and I been on your trail ever since."

"Sorry," said Lee, and though he lowered the book his forefinger kept the place.

No human being had come that way in four weeks, and Baldy knew it. Therefore he pushed back his hat, and his head was as red as his face while he considered whether or not this indifference were an insult, and if he should take it up as such. He debated, glowering upon the bent head of Lee Garrison. But, after all, it was a man's privilege to sit silent like a fool owl on a post when a chance of conversation came his way. In a word, the line rider was a nut, and not to be judged according to the standards of ordinary men. Baldy turned on his heel and without further attempt at speech unloaded his cargo and dumped it beside the dugout.

"What you want next time?" he snapped out when the last box was deposited.

"Nothing," answered Garrison, and then roused himself a little. No matter how odd a man may be in Texas he cannot safely forget all obligations of hospitality. "Maybe you're hungry?" he suggested lamely.

"I ain't."

"Or needin' a smoke?"

"I ain't."

It gave Baldy infinite satisfaction to demonstrate his own powers of curtness.

"Or thirsty?"

"Eh?"

"There's some water—"

"Water? The devil!"

Garrison sighed with relief and returned with pacified conscience to the book. Here Baldy remembered in the nick of time the most important detail of his errand to the line rider.

"I brought out another hoss for you," he said.

There was no answer.

"Nice sleepy ol' hoss," continued Baldy invitingly.

He himself and five others of the outfit had been pitched from the saddle by that same dull-eyed outlaw and now, as usual, the foreman sent his intractable mount to the line rider. For it was a well-established and significant detail of Garrison's reputation that he had never been thrown, at least not to the knowledge of those who had seen him work for five years in the Llano Estacado.

Baldy looked back at the old brown horse which stood with drooping head tethered behind the wagon. Its lower lip hung pendulous, and it slept where it stood, but at the sight a sharp pain ran through the left shoulder and hip of the cow-puncher and his face puckered at the reminiscence. He would have sold his shop-made boots for a quarter to see this silent fool in the saddle on yonder brown horse; he would have given away his vast sombrero with a joyous heart if he could have driven back to the ranch and told the boys how the dummy was thrown on his head. But Garrison had heard the news without stirring.

"Ol' hoss is tied up behind the wagon right now," went on Baldy with insidious smoothness. "Which you wouldn't

21

mind having him handy for saddling like that, would you? No work roping him, nor nothing. He's jest all handy."

The import of this drifted from afar into the ears and finally into the consciousness of Lee Garrison. He put down his book with a sigh, lifted his saddle and bridle, and climbed from the dugout. As for Baldy, he masked a smile by rubbing the back of his hand across his mouth while he made his eyes wide, childishly innocent. The brown horse was one of those rare outlaws which have not the slightest objection to the weight of a saddle. Lee Garrison, with his saddle over his arm, paused in front of the sleepy head and looked long and earnestly at the new candidate for his string.

"Does he guess?" whispered Baldy. "Pray heaven he don't guess! He don't!"

This last came in the nature of an outburst of thanksgiving, for the line rider stepped carelessly to the near side of the brown and tossed his saddle upon it with such lack of precaution that the stirrup rapped the ribs of the horse loudly. But the outlaw only canted one long, mulish ear forward and opened the opposite eye. Baldy quivered with silent delight.

"Don't let there be no warning," he continued in solemn invocation. "Let 'er hit like lightning at noon!"

The "dummy" had foot in stirrup, and now it came—a creaking of leather, a snort, a winged leap into the air, and then came the thudding impact of four hoofs with four stiff legs above them and an arched back topping it all. The brown horse came down with its head between its forelegs, a pyramid, with Lee sitting on the apex.

After that Baldy snatched his hat from his head, twisted it into a knot, and flung it on the ground. He went through odd motions, swaying from side to side, stiffening suddenly, jerking his hands in, pitching them out, like a cheerleader rousing a rooting section to frenzy, pushing the home team over the goal line. Presently he stood frozen in his last awkward attitude.

"My heaven," whispered Baldy reverently. "My heaven!"

The evening went rapidly into the twilight, the prairie dogs came out to watch, the bull bat sat silently on the fence post. Then the unrhythmic beat of hoofs ceased.

"It's true," gasped out Baldy. "I seen it—with my own eyes."

The line rider came back, passed the driver of the chuck wagon without a word, brushed the perspiration from his forehead, sat down, sighed, and then picked up his book as one in a dream. Baldy gaped at him, and then he walked away so softly that one might have said he went tiptoe over the sand.

When he started on the homeward journey he took the brown outlaw back with him.

3

THE lantern burned clear, and Garrison was content. Before him stretched a lengthy maze of adventures, jousts, waylayings, challenges; half a dozen full evenings of readings before he came to the quests of the Holy Grail and the breaking of that peerless fellowship of the Round Table; but tonight he was reading of the crisp early days when Camelot was a new name. He raised his head from the book only once; it was only to feel the settling down of utter night.

For he had learned that there is an instant of white magic just at the end of the evening. Perhaps it is the time when the creatures which see in the dark come into their own. That moment had come when Lee lifted his head. The silence which camped on the stake plains became a listening thing with a heartbeat somewhere in it; the breeze lifted the corner of the page like an invisible finger. So ended the dull day, and the night began with a breathless pause as when a door opens, but those within are not yet seen. The world died with the day, and the people of the books sprang into life. Ladies who, in the day, were bland names, became on such a night, brilliant realities with infinite life of smiles and glances. About the lonely castle he now saw the wilderness sweeping in green waves like a sea, covering the walls with a spray of vines. So solemn became the illusion of that moment that the figure which loomed in the doorway and stood there, swaying, seemed only an intruder in the dream.

Between an American Indian and an Arthurian legend, however, there existed a gap sufficient to shock Garrison into wakefulness. It was a broad-shouldered, bowlegged fellow in moccasins, with a hickory shirt, a hat set so far toward the back of his head that it pushed his ears forward, and, dangling to his shoulders, were two plaits of hair wrapped in red flannel, with a red snapper at each end. He supported himself with his hands against the door, glaring at the white man and leaning in as though he were about to leap on the prostrate figure. That illusion lasted long enough to bring Lee Garrison to his feet with the speed of a snake uncoiling. Then he saw that the poor fellow had braced himself against a staggering weakness. His arms shook under the weight they supported, and the glare of his eyes was that inward light of suffering long endured.

After a single glance at this man Garrison caught him under the armpits and swung him down to the floor of the dugout. It was a dead weight that he lifted. The shoulders of the Indian gave under the pressure of an ugly limpness, and

24

he remained in exactly the position in which Garrison deposited him; shouldering against the wall with one leg twisted oddly to the side and his right hand doubled against the floor, the weight of the arm falling against the back of the wrist. In spite of the fiery eyes of the Indian, Lee knew that the man was dying. He ripped away a stack of cans from a corner. They tumbled with a prodigious racket across the floor and revealed the hidden treasure, a half-emptied flask of whisky, which he handed to the Indian.

But the fingers in which the man tried to grasp it slipped from the glass as though numb with cold, and his arm fell. Garrison, shuddering at the sight of that mortal weakness, placed the flask at the lips of the Indian, and when he took it away the bottle was empty.

"Good!" sighed the other, and he had strength enough to take the cup of water which Lee poured.

"I have stayed too long," said the Indian in an English so perfectly enunciated that Lee started. "I must go on again."

He spread his hands on either side of him and strove to raise his body. There was no result, and a shadow dropped across his eyes. Perspiration glistened on his coppery forehead, but he smiled at the white man.

"For heaven's sake, lie down and take it easy," said Lee.

The other shook his head. There was a bubbling huskiness in the voice in which he explained gravely: "I am hollow inside and filled with fire. If I lie down it will run into my head and burn me up."

"A very good idea," said Lee quietly. "A fellow can fool fire that way, now and then. Give me your hand, will you?"

He took the languid wrist. The skin was hot; the pulse ran faint and fast as the ticking of a clock. The Indian was dying of pneumonia.

"I'm sorry I've finished your whisky stock," said he. "I'll

bring you out a new supply when I come back this way. My name is John Ramps."

Lee mumbled his own name in acknowledgment of the introduction. It would be morning before he could go to the ranch and return with help, and long before morning John Ramps would be dead.

"Moonshine will think I've left his trail," said the Indian. "But though Moonshine is clever, one can't expect a horse to know what goes on inside the brain of a man. He could run faster than my horses ran, and naturally he doesn't think I can overtake him on foot."

The feet of John Ramps were clad in moccasins, worn to shreds.

"Is Moonshine a horse?" asked Lee.

"You don't know him? Well, this is far from his home country. There were eight of us with horses when we took the trail of Moonshine in the Diamond Star Desert."

"But that's in Idaho, Ramps!" cried Garrison.

"Yes, a long trail. However, I'm surprised that you don't know of Moonshine, Mr. Garrison. He's a silver-gray mustang. You've seen moonlight running on water? That's his color. Fire in a wind, galloping across a stubble field, that's the way he runs. Now I must go. Moonshine thinks I have lost him. All the others who have tried have lost. Even Handsome Harry Chandler lost. He took his best horse. And last he rode his black mare. But even Laughter could not turn Moonshine. So he thinks that John Ramps, too, has failed. He does not know that I can still run as fast as the wind.

He lurched to his feet, but at the first step he crumpled into the arms of the white man, and Lee laid him on the blanket. He thought, then, that the end had come, for there was no perceptible breathing, but he found, at length, a faint flutter of the heart. He sponged the face and breast and hands of the man and then sat beside John Ramps to wait for the final rattle of breathing. Literally the dying man was a frame of bones loosely covered with skin. His mouth was fallen ajar, but to Lee Garrison there was nothing repulsive in the face. It took him back to the quests of Arthur's paladins after the Holy Grail. They must have ridden like this, day and night, wasting themselves to shadows, burned by their desire for one glimpse of salvation. Even so the Indian and his eight companions had ridden a thousand miles, killing their horses under them, no doubt, until only this man remained of the eight. He had spurred his last mount until it died, and then, half mad with weariness and the hysteria of fever, he had gone on by foot.

The Indian spoke. It was not the death rattle, but a harsh phrase of Indian dialect. The voice went on, detached, broken, but now it spoke English.

"Who stays to throw water when the forest burns? John Ramps is burning for the horse!"

There followed a burst of rapid chatter in his own tongue; the next English words made only a few phrases: "Let her go to another wickiup; I cannot stay."

Here he fell into inaudible mutterings, rolling his head from side to side and plucking aimlessly at his breast. Then: "Be not afraid. It is not Tahquits pounding the bones of a victim. The hoofs of Moonshine make the thunder, and John Ramps is on his back."

Was it weeks, months, even years, perhaps, since John Ramps started on the trail of the stallion? The chase was as strange to Lee as the story of the Grail. It was stranger, for in the years of his riding on the ranges he had found in horses only creatures to be subdued by main force, whipped into obedience, crushed with the stronger hand. A sullen anger came in him at the thought that a dumb beast had been able to kill this man; and also he felt a pang that the Indian could have responded to a spark that had never touched him; could have risked his life with so open a hand for the sake of a beast.

The Indian spoke again, and his voice was lower and harsher; the breath seemed to die between every dragging syllable.

"Brothers, it was no fault in the trap; the trap was good, but he is like his name—he is like Moonshine, and he eludes us. A man can take fire on two sticks and carry it through the wind; or he can gather water in his hands; or he can even put the wind in a bag and keep it; but who can gather moonshine?"

The picture Lee Garrison saw was the narrow, yellow triangle of a camp fire and eight swarthy faces glittering by that light. A sudden shout from John Ramps made his hair bristle. The Indian had jerked himself to a sitting posture, and his face was a frenzy.

"Ho! We have him. My mountain sheep, my red beauty, faster, faster! Hei!"

Over his head he swung one arm, a gesture so vivid that the whirling loop of the lasso flashed like a shadow across the eye of Lee. The hand fell; the body pitched back, and Lee, leaning close over a face which was contorted in the last agony, heard a whisper: "He is gone!"

The same whisper, it seemed, drained the last life from John Ramps, for almost at once a mist brushed across the fiery eyes as though the lamp which shone down on them had grown suddenly dim, and a gradual smile stole across the lips of John Ramps. Perhaps, thought the cow-puncher, the soul of the Indian was already flying down the trail of Moonshine and saw the fugitive.

4

IT seemed to Lee, as he looked down to the eternal triumph of that smile, that the most opulent cattle kings did not build as well as John Ramps, for their names would last only as long as the fortune held together. But John Ramps, building nothing, had left a thing that would never die, a story of which he was a part. He died for the sake of it, and as long as men loved horses they would not cease to thrill when they heard how the Indian trailed the gray stallion a thousand miles across the mountains. Here, in a bronze skin, was the type of a Galahad. Lee went to the door of the dugout. The moonlight lay in pale waves over the rolling ground outside. There was not a sound. He thought back a little. The cattle range had been a joyless place to him, a drab region, but it had at least given him escape from people and provided him with a great blessing—silence. As he stood there he grew sad with the desire to be among men. He had lived among them with his eyes closed, for there must be others in whom burned the fire of John Ramps. Perhaps with patient searching he could find one such and buckle that man to him for a friend.

In the meantime he must bury the Indian. Here on the plains was the place for him, lying face up, not too far away from this same moonlight.

He picked up the body of John Ramps, a withered body of bones and skin, and fifty yards from the dugout he placed it in a deep crevice among the rocks. Prying against the keystone of the overhanging boulders he loosed and sent down a ponderous shower of rock. The roar of the fall filled his ears for a moment longer, and then the peace of the

29

desert washed like a wave about him. In a near-by Spanish dagger the wind was whispering; that was the end. All trace of John Ramps was gone from the face of the earth, and only one man knew his monument.

Then, as though a voice from behind bade him turn, he swung sharply and saw what seemed a cloud of moonlight gathered into a moving form, half shadow, half mist, half brilliance. It glided over a hilltop, disappeared in the wash of shade that filled a gully, and slipped into view again over a closer rise of ground. It was Moonshine.

If he had never heard of the stallion before, the name would have burst from his lips as it did now in a shout. Moonshine stopped with a suddenness that sent his mane tumbling forward in a flurry of silver, and stood fast, a creature of light.

He neighed like a challenge, or a gloating over the dead man, then whirled and fled. Oh, the swing and lightness of that stride—like a wave in the free ocean!

Perhaps the soft surface sand buried the noise of hoofs. Like a phantom the wild horse drifted over the hill and faded into the shadow below.

He came into view again on a farther rise; then Moonshine was absorbed in the heart of the night. The face of Lee Garrison was like that of one who struggled to keep alive in his memory a dying music.

It was hard to turn back, for a power drew him down the trail of the horse. He closed his eyes. At once against the black of his vision the form of Moonshine stood out, luminous silver.

He had found his passions so entirely inside the covers of books that this reality, taking him by the throat, bewildered him. Had the soul of John Ramps come into his body? It was the memory of the mustang's gallop that maddened him; to

30

sit on that back would be to sit like a leaf in a level wind.

Between his knees he could sense the lithe, strong barrel of Moonshine; and his face was hot with longing to feel the wind of Moonshine's galloping.

He found himself in the dugout with his head between his hands. His face was hot; the fingers against his face were cold; his heart fluttered in a strange, airy manner; but when he sprang up his mind at least was clear.

This note he scrawled: "I got a hurry call, and I am gone." This, with some perishables which could not be trusted without guard in the dugout, he put into the saddlebags, after cinching up Pinto. When he had cut the hobble ropes the little horse, true to his homing instinct, darted toward the ranch house. So with the bridges burned Lee turned back to the dugout and swept together the necessaries. Since he had to travel on foot he cut his list of essentials to the bone. In a minute, at most, he was striding across the sand.

A cartridge belt slung over his shoulder carried his ammunition, and it supported at the lower end of the loop the heavy Colt .45. To catch a horse without a rope is nearly impossible. Lee bore thirty feet of it. A saddle blanket for shelter at night, some sulphur matches, a small package of salt, a great, powerful knife with one razor edge and another blade which defied the thickest tin can, these made up his pack, together with some odds and ends which included that prime essential of the cattle country, pliers, the key to the barbed-wire region.

It would not have been too much to carry over even fairly firm roads, but the sand melted like quicksilver under his feet, for he wore the small-soled, sharp heeled boots of the cattleman, which give the smallest walking surfaces. The heels sank deep, and in the midst of each stride there was a giving and slipping back. His eye had formed the horseman's habit of wandering forward across the landscape at the pace of a lope, and now his glances pulled him forward as though he were leaning against the wind. There is a quick, soft step for sand, barely breaking the surface as the foot falls, Indian fashion; but Lee was fighting ahead, slipping, stumbling.

The night was cool, yet Lee in ten minutes was dripping, and he sighed in ardent relief as the sand shelved to a shore of firm ground. He had reached the Capped Rock, where, the ground having settled on one side of a fissure, a ridge of broken stone protrudes along the fault, and great boulders tumble from the plateau to the lower level. From the upper ridge he scanned the dimmer regions below him anxiously.

Something winked far off like a bit of water exposed to the moon. The silvery shape dissolved in the shadows of another hollow. It seemed a mad thing for a man to start out to walk down a horse—and such a horse as Moonshine above all! Indeed the stallion might shake off all pursuit by one great burst across the country, fifty miles of running, say, which would effectually destroy all hopes of keeping the trail. Yet there was small fear that Moonshine would be so full of heart after a thousand-mile hunt across the mountains. The Indians had served one purpose by their long trailing; they had taken the edge off the mustang's wildness, and they had blunted his fear of man.

Many times, lately, he must have had the scent of a man in his wide nostrils, and many times he must have shaken off the horror with a small burst of galloping. Probably he would do the same with Lee, just keeping out of the danger distance. In that case there was one chance in three, the cow-puncher thought, of success; for the stallion would hardly have shaken off his pursuer and settled down to graze when once more the man would plod within sight and Moonshine must be off again; and hardly would he lie down to sleep when again the man scent would drift close. The gray must sleep on his feet, and even then he would only have an opportunity for brief dozes. As for Lee, he could choose his time for rest and make his sleep brief; and he had all the advantages of the general who takes the offensive and keeps the opponent guessing. All of this went swiftly through the mind of the cow-puncher, and then he started down among the rocks.

5

FOR all the pleasant ease of the first few steps on the firm ground, he quickly discovered that even the sand was preferable to this going, for sharp-edged rocks bruised his feet through the thin soles, and his spurs caught and clanked on every projecting stone. Moreover, the scrupulously shop-made boots gave no play at heel or instep, and he lumbered and halted in his stride. A sensation of prickling heat about the heel told him that the skin was chafing away. But a snug shoe and a horse with a long rein, these had been his two dominant requirements for so long that he had come to think of his body as necessarily terminating in boots. The yipping of a coyote mocked him as he paused and stared gloomily on the bright spurs, and the barking made him think of the coyote's fluffy fur and how it would feel against his aching feet. The cry of the little hunter was coming down the wind, for otherwise Lee could never have come within a mile of the wanderer's acute nose, but now Lee took covert in a brake of scrub cedar and heard the yelping coming straight at him.

The wind had blown a black slit across the hollow, and

against this darkness the light-yellow body of the skulker appeared plainly a moment later. He trotted with his head low, for since the wind was at his back the coyote had to trust to the treacherous ground smells, distinguishing nicely between the new and the old, foe and friend, that which would hunt, that which might be hunted. Two rope lengths from Lee he stopped and stood alert. Whatever sixth sense warned him, the coyote let reason outweigh intuition, and instead of changing his course at once he pointed his slender nose and raised his cry. The bark of Lee's revolver turned it into a sharp squeak; the yellow body shot high, struck the earth again with an audible impact, and lay wonderfully limp and thin.

As he ripped off the skin from the hot form, snorting the pungent odor out of his nostrils, Lee Garrison could only pray that Moonshine would be spending much of this night in sleep. The fresh pelt would be useless until it was at least partially dried, so he cut four small cedar branches to stretch the hide and fastened it securely at his back. There it must dry as he walked.

The pause allowed his feet to puff, but after the first few tortured steps the pressure shut off the circulation of the blood; presently all feeling ceased below the ankles. There was only the ache of leg muscles protesting against this unaccustomed exercise.

He went on. The soreness grew; the aches accumulated and sprang out in surprising places; but he set himself a measured pace and kept at it with monotonous effort. He felt certain that the stallion must have followed a cut through certain low hills, far ahead, and to this goal he pointed. If pain were the price of Moonshine, he was beginning to pay in generous installments.

Now black mountains began to grow out of the horizon,

seeming to drift toward him. The sky turned from full silver to a ghostly mist, fog-colored—dawn was coming. With that, weariness struck him squarely between the eyes, and he knew he must make a halt.

Skirting into a cedar brake he saw the nervous head and topknot of a blue Mexican quail, and shot it. He dressed the quail swiftly and placed it over a fragrant flame on cedar branches. As long as he could, he endured the odor of the roasting meat, and then he devoured his meal half raw.

The day was quickening, now, the sky blue, the east fresh with color; a few breaths of that keen, clear air drove the ache of sleeplessness from his brain, and he started again toward the pass among the tumbling hills.

In the firm sand of the pass he found the small prints of Moonshine as clear as print on a white page, and, with his revolver, he measured the steps accurately, scratching the odd distance on the barrel of his gun. By this measure, better than by any other method, he could identify the stallion's trail.

As he hurried on, it seemed to Lee that out of the prints before him the body of the horse arose and drifted before him with rhythmic pace.

During the day he halted only twice, for after a pause it became more than a man could endure to stop again on those agonizing feet. That straightforward progress brought a reward, however. He came on Moonshine beside a water hole near plenty of long grass which the stallion was eating so eagerly that Lee guessed how famine pinched him. For his own part, as the gray raced off into the evening, he had barely strength to stagger to the edge of the hole. There he dropped into the mud and drank the lukewarm water. Afterward, it was vain to attempt to drag his boots off over those swollen feet, so he cut away the leather below the ankles and tossed spurs and all far off. One glance at his feet, and he buried them in the mud. It was a green slime, unspeakably soft, cool. It drank up the fever of his blood; it cleared his head; it drained away the thousand aches while he lay flat on his back, breathing with a hoarse rattle of content, his arms thrown out crosswise, staring up to the evening sky where the colors were mingling softly and gayly.

There, with his feet in the mud, he took the half-dried skin of the coyote and fashioned moccasins. A double fold of skin made the soles; the uppers were crudely shaped and joined to the sole with a strip of sinew passed through holes which he cut with his knife. That done, in the gathering darkness he lay back and waited until a blue quail came fearlessly to the water and killed it.

It was painful going in the morning; but he kept at it gingerly along a trail that was as clear as if it had been stamped out. He reached the Pecos Country that day, with the great brown mountains growing up beyond to the white snow that topped Guadalupe. The rolling land swept into a great vega, and in the midst of it he stumbled upon the river. A few rods back it was not visible; and when he reached the famous stream he found little three-foot banks hemming in a swift, muddy current no broader than a street. He forded that bitter water at the Delaware Crossing and went on into a sandy country.

The sign led toward the Guadalupe until at night, at the base of the great mountain which now filled a quarter of the sky, the trail swung sharply to the right. It made Lee Garrison draw a deep breath of relief. Moonshine had traveled swiftly that day, and now he must lead by many a mile, but by that veering of the tracks Lee knew that the mustang was taking the ravine to the right in order to cut into the heart of the mountains. That would lead him about on a winding course, and Lee, going straight over the shoulder of the mountain, might cut across the path before Moonshine came up with him. For that reason he decided to eat his supper if he could find game, rest a brief time, and then press straight over the shoulder of the mountain.

Luck gave him his game in the form of a white-tailed buck which stood out of the short brush against the sky line not two hundred yards away. Lee stalked him as silently as a snake, and coming up out of the gully, he fired from below and dropped the deer with the first shot. It was a fine eight-point fellow running close to one hundred and fifty pounds, but all of him went to waste except the plump hind quarters. Off one of these Lee cut himself a huge steak and broiled it over cedar coals, a meal for a king. While he smoked his cigarette afterward, he watched the falling night across the plains below, while above him the air whispered through evergreen boughs, and that nameless keen fragrance was blowing. His body ached when he thought what a bed those piled branches would make! But he paused only long enough to massage his sore leg muscles with his knuckles, fasten the untouched quarter of the buck across his shoulders, and then he pressed on up the slope.

At midnight he reached a crest that seemed closer to the stars than he had ever been before, but they were visible for a moment only. A freshening wind was carrying great burdens of clouds across the sky, and the stars were flicked out one by one. In the redoubled darkness the voices of the wind crowded close to him with lonely wailing, but Lee armed himself against despondency.

He glanced back of him to make sure of his direction and then went down the slope toward the ravine along which Moonshine must surely be climbing.

A gust, as he started, struck him heavily, and instead of

slackening it increased in stronger puffs, one crowded after the other, humming and whining across the ridges and plucking at Lee Garrison with fingers of ice. Below, the valley was dark as a cave.

He was too old a cattleman to become panic-stricken at the approach of a storm, but as he went on he took stock of the swift falling of the temperature, the rapidly increasing numbness of toes and fingers, the prickling about his cheekbones. A true hurricane was in the brewing. A blast of sleet rattled through the shrubs, then clouds of snow poured about him, waving down like great moth wings and clothing the air to stifling with its density. It seemed that he would never stagger to the bottom of the first descent.

A moment later, however, he came into that ravine which, he knew, must be the course of Moonshine as he crossed the Guadalupes. The level-driving snow literally roofed the gorge, but he could see for a little distance up and down. Behind an outcropping of rock he crouched to wait, straining his eyes down the hollow for some sign of the stallion. It might be that Moonshine had turned with the gale and drifted as cattle drift, but Lee had strong faith that in spite of wind and weather the gray would keep to his course like a thinking man. The cold mountains went by. Drifts of sheeted snow from time to time blew past him like ghosts, or galloping gray horses, and his heart leaped at so many false hopes that he would not believe when, out of the snow flurries below him, he made out a moving shape which grew into the mustang struggling through the storm on his journey north, steady as a ship which drives by compass.

He slid his hand back and gripped the coil of the rope. Gallantly Moonshine came up the rise until, just in front of Lee, an arm of the wind shot sidewise and stopped the horse like a jerk of a stake rope. Lee Garrison shook out the noose a little. He lurched up and forward for the cast. But his body crumbled under the effort. The cold had made him as brittle as straw, for he had crouched by the rock too long. His legs buckled at the knees. The rope was caught by the wind and flung back into his face while the horse leaped past him with a snort, almost within the reach of his finger tips.

To tantalize him the more, he regained muscular control at once. The strong effort now sent his blood leaping. He sprang to his feet and rushed down the ravine shouting, shaking the rope above his head. The storm tore off his curses at his lips. He stumbled and fell flat a dozen times. But he kept on until he heard, far away, the storm-drowned neigh of Moonshine. Then, with a groan, he crumpled up on a bank of snow.

6

THAT failure in the pass among the snows, seemed as definite an end as the falling of the curtain on the last act of a tragedy. Yet he found himself mechanically plodding on through the storm with no more hope than one driven on a treadmill by a whip. Half frozen, feeble, despairing, he descended from the peak until a sudden wind tore the clouds to tatters and let through a hearty burst of sunshine. Garrison took it as a sign from heaven, and in half an hour he was singing on the northward trail of Moonshine.

It was well that he could not look into the future. But every night when he lay down it was with a hope, and every morning when he stood up it was with a hope. He labored across the rugged Pinasco country, a continual up and down of ravines, wading through icy creeks up to the waist and struggling up a succession of weary slopes through thickets of dewberries and wild blackberries which the bears come down to eat. He slept short watches, dropping down in wet or dry, hard or soft, wherever his strength failed him, and wakened again by a sure alarm—a feeling of impending loss. Sometimes on the march he grew light-headed and found himself in strange surroundings, having walked miles and miles, following the trail with a subconscious attention. For food he had the quarter of the deer for a time, eked out with the wild, red haws with their crab-apple flavor, a delicious novelty. When the venison became rank he killed where and what he could, never deviating from the sign of Moonshine in order to hunt game.

So he came to the valley of the Rio Grande, gaunt, sun-blackened, but with a spirit edged like a keen appetite. His body was starved to lightness, but his eyes blazed out of a shadow as though in passing through the fire he had carried some of it away with him. And indeed never a day passed without one glimpse of Moonshine, a golden moment which was enough to carry him on with a high head. But from the brow of a mesa in the Rio Grande, on this great day, he had at last a long view and a clear view of the stallion. The face of the mesa dropped to a wild tangle of willows beneath, and from the farther side of the trees the gray horse trotted into the flat beside the river.

To Garrison that sight of the silver beauty was as a glimpse of the Grail to the starved soul of Lancelot. Tears of joy misted his eyes. He brushed the moisture away to see the stallion pause, turn his head into the wind to reconnoiter some distant danger, perhaps, and then trot ahead. He aimed at a place where the river wound in an oxbow loop, a loop wide at the belly, but close together at the neck.

Here Lee Garrison leaped to his feet and stood trembling

with a thought. Suppose that winding current were swifter than Moonshine anticipated, too swift to be forded? Then when the horse turned from the edge of the stream, suppose that Lee could gain the throat of the loop and block the retreat?

He slid down the face of the mesa by swinging himself from one projecting bush to another or letting himself shoot down a sandy slope. At the bottom he ran like an Indian, weaving among the trees until a distant sound like the rumbling of a heavy wagon across a bridge stopped him. It might be thunder, yet as far as he could see, the sky was clear of a cloud. Moreover, there was this difference; it was not a single boom or a succession of noises, but a steady roar which grew in volume perceptibly during the moment he stood there. Then he understood. He had heard that same grumbling before, up some river valley, and at length had seen a solid wall of water rush down the ravine, tearing up old trees as it went, ripping out banks, filling the valley with thunder. A sudden downpour of rain in mountains might cause it, or the breaking of a natural dam. Suppose that speeding wave struck Moonshine as the stallion was swimming?

As he raced out of the willows he saw his nightmare realized. Down the river came a bluff front of foam and thunder with stripped tree trunks jumping in it like little sticks in the hands of a juggler. Moonshine was galloping toward the farthest arc of the circle, thoroughly within the trap, for, unless he crossed the stream before that tidal wave swept past, he would be hemmed in by the tremendous current which followed that moving ridge of water. And here was Lee Garrison, pausing for breath in the mouth of the loop, swinging his rope and opening the noose! He heard a great rending and crashing up the river bed and saw a line of willows near the bank shaved away and juggled like straws in the waters. Nothing could live in that torrent; a freak of the current tossed a long trunk into the air, javelin-wise.

Even the stallion seemed appalled, but turning to retreat he saw Lee blocking that narrow pass. He stopped a moment with head high, his tail and mane flaunted in the wind. Then he came like a bullet straight at the man. A bull closes its eyes before it strikes, but a horse keeps his eyes wide open, and when a mustang runs amuck, guns are in order. Dodging is practically impossible. Lee Garrison jerked up his revolver, caught the silver head in the sights, and dropped the gun. He could not shoot. He swung the lariat, prepared for a leap to one side as he cast the rope. The stallion came on like a thing made of light until Lee swayed forward to make his cast. Then Moonshine veered. A spray of sand shot into the face of the cow-puncher and the gray was racing straight back down the loop, neighing as he ran.

It had been an Indian charge, an attempt to conquer through fear, and it left Lee shaken and cursing with relief and admiration. But the feint at the man had taken desperately needed time. Now the white wall was ripping its way with thunder around the upper corner of the loop. A spray of white shot high in the air as, in its straight course down the river bed, it smashed against the bank not six yards from him. The ground shook beneath him and the roar stunned his ears; then, as a dense rain showered upon him, the water bank veered to the right and lurched along the upper side of the loop. The stallion ran for the ford with his head turned, watching the progress of that shouting torrent as it leaped and rolled and foamed and tossed the trees it had uprooted. Lee dropped the rope, cupped his hands in his mouth, and into the uproar shrieked his warning. He might as well have tried to throw a straw against a sixty-mile gale.

The wave was rounding the upper corner of the loop when Moonshine shot from the bank into the muddy stream, disappeared, and came up halfway across the water with pricking ears. Gallantly he swam, making a wake behind him, but now the water about him shuddered into little waves before the coming of the flood. Lee dropped to his knees and covered his eyes, digging his nails into his face.

The thundering overwhelmed even his thoughts. It filled his mind as the sun fills the heavens. Then it seemed that through the roaring pierced a long, hoarse cry, like the scream of a horse dying in agony. And now the moving wall of destruction roared away, bearing his picture of the dead body, tumbled in the waters, to be washed on the banks far below. He dreaded so to look on the truth that he had to fight his hands down from his face. Yonder stood Moonshine on the farther bank, dripping with water, and, in the sun, too brilliant to be looked upon. He whirled and raced off, a flowing form of light. The knot in the throat of Lee was loosened, and through him passed a great weakness of thanksgiving.

He could not follow until the flood subsided. Therefore he built a fire and, pouring water into a hole in a rock, he heated it with stones from the fire and made sagebrush tea. In this he soaked his sore feet, and while he sat there he was deep in his tattered "Malory." The tales which he read now by preference were those which he had once shunned with a half physical aversion, the adventures of the quest of the Grail. At the end of each day's march, indeed, he propped his eyes open a little longer to read of Percivale and the black horse, or how Lionel fought with Bors, his brother. Sometimes he looked down from his reading at his wasted brown fingers, thin as the hands of a hermit. At such moments he wondered at himself. This day, when he closed the book and rose for the trail, he had lost the hope of capturing the stallion, but the quest itself, if the differentiation can be understood, was more a burning part of him than ever.

The labor of the pursuit itself grew less, for though he climbed out of the valley of the Rio Grande and soon struck the lofty Mogollon Mountains and a forest of virgin pine, he was hardened to his work; he knew how to measure himself; at what pace to climb, and how to save himself through the heat of the day for a greater effort in the evening. The sign was always fresh, now, for Moonshine, robbed of rest, hard pressed to find fodder as he traveled, weakened rapidly. In the distance Lee noted the lean rump, and sometimes he even saw the shadows of the ribs of starvation. It gave him a peculiar pain to see what he was accomplishing, and yet he pressed on relentlessly. And so he came out of the Mogollons and reached the lava beds.

Black rock flowed to the end of the world. There were bits and even long stretches of glassy stuff, maddening to walk on, or rutted and ridged places terrible for moccasined feet. Again there were expanses like coal cinders made of blown glass, endless acres of petrified coke, and domes as large as huge haystacks as if there the molten rock had bubbled up, and solidified before it could fall. In that black wilderness he made no attempt to follow the trail, but merely gave himself to a desperate effort to win across before night. That afternoon he recklessly exhausted his canteen and his strength. Yet the evening found him still struggling with bruised feet among those endless mounds of burned stone, and he submitted to the inevitable sorrow that was to come.

The cinders were better for a bed than the rock. He scraped a quantity of them together, levelled them off, and scattered his pack upon them. But no sleep came to him that night. No matter how he wrapped himself, the wind that hisses among the rocks found its way to his skin, parching him, drying his throat to parchment. He forced a swallow at regular intervals to keep his throat partially moist, and each swallow was a greater effort, until his muscles ached. There seemed nothing vivifying in that wind, as though the oxygen had been robbed from it, so that he had to fight back a continual desire to open his mouth wide and gape down the air in great mouthfuls. He dared not do it. An instant's gulping of the cold wind would parch his mouth until the tongue puffed and cracked at last. All the night he regulated his breathing and fought away the panic as it surged at him. Overhead the stars were bright in a dim, steel-blue heaven, and they burned down closer and closer, to watch him. They started the panics, those cyclike stars.

Dawn came. He had prayed for it. Then he roused out of a stupor and found the stars dim, the sky gray. The day was beginning. He sat up, dropped his face between his hands, and thought. If he turned back the way he had come, he knew that he could last out the journey and gain the last spring from which he had drunk in the mountainside. If he went on, there was an unknown stretch of the lava flow. Unless he crossed it before darkness he would die. But to turn back meant the end of all hopes of taking Moonshine. Tales of the book drifted through his memory, knights who had quested till they came to the very gates of discovery, and then turned away conquered by their own weak hearts. At last he took up his pack with trembling hands, set a course as well as he could by the cool, blue Zuni Mountains south and east, and started.

The sun came up red, huge, without heat, and, drifting a little above the horizon, was lost in a sheeting of gray clouds.

There it stayed all the day, small and dim as a moon, and left the world below to a wind which had grown in violence during the night. Now it whined among the rocks full in Lee's face. He became childishly sullen, as though the gale had been directed to that quarter of the compass by a personal malignancy. Worst of all, it forced down his nostrils a stinging dust that was invisible to the eye but burned his throat and stifled him with a peculiarly pungent odor. Several times he had to turn his back to the wind to take an easy breath.

By the middle of the morning the gale had increased, but it ceased to take any scruple of the thoughts of Lee Garrison. His mind was fully occupied by a morbid study of the thirst that burned in him. In the first hour of walking his tongue had begun to puff, and the effort of keeping his mouth closed nearly stifled him, but worse than that was the torment of his throat and the terrible effort of swallowing. It was about noon, or thereabouts, that he stopped short, realizing that he could not swallow again. His throat was numb with the vain struggle. The panic which was ever just at his shoulder now leaped on him, and his reason staggered.

Only a little more and he would plunge into gibbering idiocy. He thrust his hand in front of his eyes and studied the fingers as he wiggled them slowly back and forth. All the tortures of thirst were nothing compared to that fear of the insanity which comes with it. Another instant and the hallucinations would begin with daydreams of fountains of crystal-cold water; of mountains of snow; of delectable berries, frosted and juicy; of endless bottles of icy wine. Then he would see a blue lake in the middle of the desert, a lake so real that the waves rolled in and broke with a shower of spray upon the shore.

And with the dead aches in his throat he tried to occupy

his mind by remembering long quotations from "Malory," but always those quotations began to repeat themselves automatically, meaninglessly, and the whole force of his mind, he would discover suddenly, was fixed on a dream of the snowstorm in the Guadalupes. Ah, if such a storm should come now he would walk with his head bent far back and let the great, luscious flakes pour into his open mouth! He would sweep them to his lips with both hands!

Here his sane self wakened Lee from a trance in which he actually walked with his head far back, his mouth gaping wide. It had been a narrow escape. The perspiration started out all over his weakened body as he realized how close the peril had come, and he forced his bleeding feet into a run. Yet the thought of escape by flight was in itself madness! He stopped. He sank his teeth in his forearm and sucked the crimson substance. And that gave him the power to draw one free breath and swallow again.

Out of the torture that followed he remembered two things. Once he looked behind him and saw that a red trail led up to him made by his own lacerated feet. And again there was a crisis during which he seriously considered lancing the swollen tongue which choked him. He balanced that thought soberly for a time, walking with the open knife in his hand.

Coming out of another haze, he noticed that he was seeing the lava hummocks farthest ahead of him against a background of light gray, the desert stretched before him. He shouted—it was only a hoarse, gagging murmur—and the black nightmare vanished. Then he dropped to his knees, scooped up the sand, and let it fall back through his fingers, laughing aloud.

It was hearing that horrible, small laughter that sobered him to the understanding that though sand were preferable to stone, he was still far from water, and ten days' searching might not find it. What would Moonshine, himself, do? He had a gift like other wild horses, doubtless, and would scent water far off. On this hint he builded. If he could find Moonshine's trail, it might lead him to safety. As well look for the paths of the stars in the seas, however, as try to find the trace of his footprints in this sand which ran like water into every depression Lee's moccasins made. A touch of wind washed the surface smooth again. With the soft sand easing the pain of his feet like a blessing, he laid his course in an S-shape, winding back and forth in the hope of striking a bit of firm ground that would hold the sign of the stallion.

He found it at last in a little island of clay among the drift sand—three hoof marks. With his knife he drew a straight line through the prints—it pointed the direction of Moonshine's flight. Even then his chance was small, for that direction might change if the horse had not actually scented water.

The sun, as if realizing that there was no longer a chance of discouraging the traveler with gray and cold, had broken through the clouds, which tumbled down to the horizon. Facing a blinding sun he struck away from the firm ground and was instantly ankle deep. As he labored on the blood swayed into his brain each time he lifted the rearward foot. It crowded behind his eye until the skull threatened to split, then ebbed, and weakness ran through him. Between the spasms of agony of breathing and walking he felt a sort of divine promise that if he endured this last test of fire Moonshine must be his. He was paying in full.

Straight before him something glittered, as though there were two suns, one in the sky and one flat on the desert. It changed to a ball of fire set in pale blue. A cloud drifted across the sun; the ball of fire grew dim among the sands. It was water, a wide, blue pool, but a miracle of spring water brimming a hollow not fifty feet away.

He went on his hands and knees until he lay at full length on the moist brim with his face buried in the pool.

7

THE sand was a tremendous handicap to Moonshine. For his small hoofs cut deep into the earth while Lee merely dusted through the surface, so to speak. And now the horse was rarely out of sight, a glimmering shape struggling through the reddish brown dirt. Sometimes, to shake off that slow, plodding, relentless form, the stallion burst into a gallop; but a few minutes of it brought him back to a walk. A little later Garrison would come bobbing out of the skyline.

In the meantime the cow-puncher was seasoned to his work. He knew to perfection the short step which served him best in such going. The slipping of his feet no longer worried him, and his leg muscles were turning to iron. He passed Yacoma of the Moki Indians in their strange, semi-Oriental costumes, with their hair bobbed over their shoulders and white cotton trousers, and from them, the first human beings he had seen since the long trail began, he bought two rolls of their Indian bread with the last cent of his money. His cartridge supply was perilously low, but food was more important than bullets.

He had reason to bless that purchase, for a bitter country lay before him, swept clean of forage for Moonshine and game for man. Near Nic Doit Soe Peak a sandstorm struck him, a dull, reddish mist rolling up on the horizon and spreading until the sun itself was veiled. It had been hot, sweltering and still, but the temperature dropped fifty degrees in as many moments, and then the wind struck him with its burden of fine red silt. Only the presence of a sandstone butte behind which he took shelter, saved him that day, and how Moonshine lived through it he never would understand. But when the storm passed over, as suddenly as it had come, and the heat wave struck in behind it, he found the horse still journeying before him, red, now, instead of white.

After that came Colorado, a mile-wide gulch whose rock walls were like banks of mist with a setting sun behind them, gray-green cliffs of diorite, cold granite fogs, rhyolite, an incredible lavender-pink, everywhere benches and slides of earth, blue, yellow, purple, brown, and farther down the cañon, a naked cliff face of talc, dazzling white. That riot of pigments stretched beyond, and over miles and miles of bad lands to the north, south, and west, with the blues of evening pooled in hollows here and there, and dimming the brightest red to purple. And the stream which had done this vast piece of quarrying? Far below it lay, like a brown chalk mark scraped across the rocks.

Halfway down the cliff he paused to see the stallion emerge from the river on the farther side, the desert stain washed away, and once more a form of silver. After that glance he bent grimly to his work and came at length, panting, to the valley floor with a rush of small rocks about him. That sound near at hand, almost masked a distant rattling. He threw himself forward, heard a sound like vast wings, and then a fall that rocked the earth. The largest rocks of the landslide came skipping about him, and then the cañon walls took up the roar of that fall. As mirrors catch and repeat light, so the cliffs, angling in and out, caught the long thunder of the landslide and sent it far away. Once it quite died out, and then some projecting wall sent it sharply back and made Lee glance over his shoulder in alarm.

He was seven days in the bad lands to the north before he pulled over the crest of the Virgin Mountains and saw the Little Muddy Range beyond. That valley was a rest to him, and the climbing of the Little Muddy, on the other side, was a small matter, but when he dropped onto the lower plateau beyond, it was different.

It was well into April, now; and with the later season and the lower ground he struck the full blast of the mountain-desert heat. Like a prophecy of evil, the first living creature he met with was a sickly, gray-green horror with a flabby beaver tail, a lizard body, chameleon head, and saw teeth in its vast mouth. That evening he pumped his last three bullets at an elusive rabbit for his evening meal. After that he had desert to travel on, and rocks or sticks to knock down his game. Ten days before that prospect would have stopped him short, but now he lived like a wild beast, never looked ahead farther than one meal, and denied himself the luxury of hunger until he saw the game.

The second day he wound into the Hyko Mountains with the Silver Cañon Range thrusting out fingers from the south, and on the third day he dropped over the Hyko Mountains into the Pahroc Valley, ninety miles of desert. Through it a cloud of dust swept and dissolved into a herd of wild horses which picked up Moonshine at the foot of the hills, and then swept away from his feeble galloping.

He left the Hykos with a full canteen in the middle of the day; he reached Dry Lake that night, far up the valley, and found it dry indeed; and then, with an empty water tin, he tramped behind the glimmering form of Moonshine down the road to Coyote Wells and sank beside the watering troughs after a sixty-five-mile march.

Strength and muscle and nerve ebbed away in the time that followed. To White River, and White Pine Mountains; then a stretch of desert from the White Pines to the Buttes, and desert again from the Buttes to Hastings Pass, every day he found his march smaller, every day he roused from his sleep later, with a heavy buzzing in his ears and a mist before his eyes. Flesh began to drop away from him, not superfluous fat, which had been burned away in the first week of his march, but the vital, necessary muscle itself; his step grew shorter. Yet each morning he braced himself and threw his head high like a runner entering the home stretch, feeling it impossible that the shambling skeleton which hobbled before him, the dull, gray cartoon of horse, could last out another struggle until the dark. But always there was something left under those bones and that flabby skin which enabled Moonshine to come out of that down-headed, trailing walk into a trot and then into a laboring gallop.

It was after each vain pursuit that Lee realized he must either give up the pursuit or else lighten his load. Already he had thrown away everything except the rope, the knife, and "Malory." That night he read the book for the last time; or, rather, he sat turning the ragged, familiar leaves. He knew the creases and the tears fully as well as he knew the print. That page where Dinaden jousted with Palomides while Tristan looked on was marked with a great brown stain of rain water; and the tournament of Lonazhep was obscured by half a page torn away; a great wrinkle crossed the death scene of Balin, when he "yede" on his hands and knees to the red knight and found that he had killed his brother; and the print of Lancelot's fight with Turquin was too dim to follow, for the book had here lain face upward to the sun through the whole day.

The next morning "Malory" lay in a shallow grave

beneath a rock, and Lee went on some vital ounces lighter, but with a mournful sense of loss.

That day he pressed the mustang hard, yet his nerve was gone. He trembled like a woman when his foot slipped on a rolling pebble. He no longer tried for short cuts. Where Moonshine went he followed, up hill and down. He lived on game he could knock over with rocks, stupid mountain grouse, or the sage hens, running clumsily. Indeed, it was when he caught up a stone to throw at a grouse, that he found the gold.

As he raised his hand the morning light glittered in the quartz, a rosy, semi-transparent rock with brownish cubes in it, and all these cubes spotted and sparkling with gold. All about the hillside sparkled with the outcropping which a small landslide had stripped to the sun. A glimpse of that hill would start a gold rush. He marked the place. Above him was a higher summit crested with naked white rocks. Below him a creek twisted noisily down a rough-sided valley and carried its foam and its talking out to a level lowland.

But yonder a bony gray horse paused and looked back at Lee, one ear pricked forward and the other flagging wearily back. A childish thought came to the man; suppose the mustang had purposely led past this place to bait him with gold. He tossed up the quartz. It flashed in a rosy streak and fell heavily into his palm—heavy with gold, thought Lee. Then he saw that Moonshine had disappeared. After he had caught the horse, then there would be time for the gold. He paused only to drag his belt still tighter about his hollow waist and then stumbled on.

Till midafternoon he reeled on the down pitch or labored with groans up the rise of those endless ridges until a voice sounded just over the next crest. It had the booming quality of an echo, and he imagined for a moment that it might be his own voice; for many times before he had been startled by a sound and found that it was his own singing or talking as he walked in a dream. But now, on the edge of the ridge appeared a burro with flopping ears and patient, sagging head. Looking up from the hollow the pack seemed as big as the beast, a burden monstrous in the sky, and Lee felt that every knob and projecting corner of the pack must speak of the provisions with which it was jammed. Lee pictured a man newly out of town, with a store of syrup, yellow corn meal, snow-white flour, and bacon—oh, miracle among foods—bacon! There would be plenty of sugar for the coffee, black coffee with soul-enchanting breath; and there would be a small box of assorted cookies not yet consumed. But above all there must be a great store of tobacco of all kinds—half a dozen varieties of cigarettes, much tobacco for the pipe, and perhaps even a few cigars! His brain floated on a bright cloud of laughter, his eyes watered. But bitter disappointment cleared the dimness away, for the first glance showed that the man had been long, long on the trail. Yet even if no delicacies were left in his larder, how welcome a sight was that great bulking body, the flapping hat of soft felt, the blue shirt, dull with time and dirt, and a short pipe upside down between bearded lips. A winged angel would not have been so welcome to Lee as the sight of that pipe!

He stood right against the sky line with a huge arm thrown up in greeting, and the wind parting his black beard. He shouted a greeting, a vast voice that flooded about Lee and made his own weakness seem tenfold greater. He waved his answer and, struggling on, he stumbled and fell upon both hands. A heavy boot crunched on the gravel. An arm shot beneath him, and he was jerked erect.

"What the devil?" said the big man. "Now, what the devil?"

"Sort of—lost my balance," gasped out Lee.

"H'm!" muttered the other, "you sit down on that rock yonder and I'll fix you up some flapjacks. Darned if I ain't out of bacon and coffee, but I got a snack of flour left and a bit of grease. What you need is something in your belly, m'young friend."

A flash of gray disappeared over the next ridge. Suppose the stranger had seen and guessed the identity of that hollow-ribbed horse?

"I'm due over yonder," said Lee. "I gotta start on!"

"Oh," grunted the prospector, and his glance dropped to the polished surface where the discarded holster had played against the trousers. There is only one thing that ordinarily sends a man into the mountains without horse or weapon. "Oh," repeated the prospector. "If that's the way of it, I won't bother you, but when a gent wants to make speed, he'll save time by eatin' along the way. Speaking personal, which here's hoping you don't take it the wrong way, you look like the devil. Darned if you don't make me think of a pore old rambledly shaklety gray hoss that went dragging himself across my trail a while back. By heaven, I looked at that old skeleton and fingered my gun. I come near putting him out of his pain. You're like him—" He broke off with an enormous laugh that set Lee's nerves jumping. "Not that I was figuring on pulling a gun on you, too!"

Far off the sun glimmered again on the stallion; he was gaining mortal ground every moment. Lee would not stay for food, but tobacco? He closed his fingers over the quartz rock which he still carried until his hand ached!

"If you can give me a handful of tobacco?" he asked.

The prospector flushed to the eyes.

"If you're short," said Lee, "don't bother about me!"

"Wait," said the other huskily. He caught Lee by the shoulder as the latter started to turn away. "Wait a minute."

He was panting in his anxiety. "Three days I been nursing this here pipe along without lighting it, because it's all burned out, and because I got just one pipeful left. I been chewing the pipestem and drawing on it, kind of fooling myself."

He dug into his pocket and brought out a palm half filled with gold and silver coins.

"I got fifty dollars here that ain't doing me no good. Here's half for you. You can fit yourself out the first dump you come to, but just leave me the bit of tobacco. Is that square?"

"Sure," said Lee, "but I don't want your money."

The flush of the other turned to a deep purple.

"My name's Olie Guttorm," he said. "You ask about me in these parts and they'll tell you that I'm square. I'll split the tobacco with you fifty-fifty!"

He dragged out a battered sack, secured by many wrappings of string.

"Never mind," said Lee, and to show his indifference he tossed up the quartz and caught it again. "Never mind, Guttorm, I can get along."

But as he turned, Guttorm caught him back and froze Lee's wrist in a mighty grasp while he stared at the rock in his hand.

"Rose quartz," he murmured, "and hematite of iron, and gold in the hematite!"

His little pale-blue eyes flared at Lee. "I can see why you're in a hurry. I been bursting my heart over quartzite, breaking four inches a day, and here you come with this!" He added humbly: "Is there much in sight?"

"A whole hill of it." He spoke with his eyes on the faint horizon toward which the stallion must be moving. Only that wild hunger for tobacco auctioned him.

"Guttorm, I'll give you this sample, partner, and I'll tell

56

you where to find the rest of it. Will you hand me over that tobacco?"

Guttorm cradled the rock in both his hard hands. The tobacco had fallen to the ground.

"D'you mean it?" he cried. "D'you mean it?"

Lee stooped and picked up the tobacco. He said: "You see that tall hill away back yonder with the mountain with white rocks on top to the left? That's the place."

A thread of doubt held Guttorm: "Are they following you that close?" he asked, "and you without a gun? You can't even stop for this? A whole hill of this?"

"The sun is red on it, Guttorm!"

The prospector struck the burro a tremendous thwack that sent it scampering over the ridge. He himself followed as fast, paused on the crest and waved to Lee with a shout, then dropped out of sight.

8

BEFORE the head of Guttorm sank from sight Lee was filling his pipe, in such trembling haste that he dropped precious shreds of tobacco in the gravel. He heeded it not, for now the pipe was lighted and the first life-giving breath of smoke drawn into his lungs. It went so deep that hunger was forgotten, his brain cleared and new energy vitalized his flaccid muscles. He started again in the pursuit.

From the second ridge he sighted Moonshine in the hollow. With forelegs sprawled wide, the stallion was tearing at a bunch of sun-faded grass, and when it came up by the roots he staggered loosely. The mustang was weak as a fever-stricken child, and Lee Garrison grinned with a cruel satisfaction. He walked straight on, leisurely, until the pipe was smoked to the last cinder. Then, his body light with the strength of that stimulus, he cut around the stallion at a swift run, keeping out of sight beyond the next hill, and finally dropping down in a perfect covert among rocks which seemed to be directly in the line of the gray's march.

He had barely reached shelter when the mustang topped the ridge above and paused there, looking back down the trail, as if he sought for the familiar form of his tormentor. Moonshine was a skeleton, indeed, but his head was still proud. Then he came down the slope. Halfway along the descent he began to trot, because the steep pitch of the ground forced him forward, and he lacked the strength to brace back. Striking the level floor of the valley he staggered drunkenly, and then he headed toward the rocks where his enemy lay.

Lee went sick with excitement. He forced himself to look away until his heart stopped rioting. It was a shallow valley with the bright streak of a river in its midst, a river which pitched out of view in the distance and sent back the dull mumbling of a waterfall.

A snort from the gray made the watcher look back to the horse. The stallion had stopped very near by. His shoulders, once so smoothly, powerfully muscled, were now sharp ridges. The broad chest was hung with flabby skin. But now, as some alarm was brought vaguely to his mind, his neck arched, his ears pricked, and his eyes shone with the old unconquerable fire.

Garrison waited until those drawling feet went by—an eternity of waiting. He had even time to close his eyes and pour forth his soul in prayer. The next instant he started to his feet and threw the rope, quickly, before the tremor in his heart spread to his hand.

There was still a mysterious well from which the ruined horse drew strength. As the rope leaped past him he started into a plunging gallop. How different from that neat-footed and lightning stride which had once been his! Once he would have twisted and dodged and darted away as a snipe flies, but now he could only pound straight ahead. The noose struck the ground, and his forefoot landed inside it; Moonshine was flung heavily on his side. He whirled to scramble up again, but Lee was running in, working the rope. The lariat writhed around every leg, and Moonshine lay hopelessly entangled! One great struggle and then he was still—the quest was ended; Moonshine was captured.

Lee looked down at his brown hands with a deep wonder that there had been strength enough in them to win such a battle. A thousand pains which had tortured him on the trail now burned through him again. And a thousand hopes were now transformed into a kingdom of victory.

He stepped back to look at his prize. It was a captive body, but the spirit—ah, that was a different thing! The eye which he turned upon the man was as steady and bright as a star. For a long time they stared at one another before the glance of the beast wavered from the glance of the man. Then the gaze neither dropped nor turned, but plunged straight past and far off into the pale blue of the sky. A chill shivered through Lee Garrison. He followed that glance and saw a wavering black speck in the sky. He knew by the flight that it was an eagle.

"Dear God!" sighed Lee. "If I could make you my hoss, Moonshine!"

With the shirt from his back he made a bandage for the eyes of the mustang. Next he loosened the rope on the legs and allowed the horse to rise. Moonshine merely shook his head a little at the clinging darkness, and Lee cut the rope in

59

two, using part of it for a cinch, with bits of cloth fastened at the sides by way of stirrups. The rest he fashioned into a halter with a slip noose, so that with a strong pull he could choke the horse. A rock near by gave him a step, from which he easily swung into place on the back of the stallion. But Moonshine merely shuddered and was still.

The time had come. Lee fixed his feet in the stirrups and tore the bandage away. For a moment Moonshine did not stir; then he shot from springs, straight up. He came down with his head lowered, his feet bunched closely together, and whirled like a spinning top. Only a chance kept Lee from being slung to the ground. Thereafter he found himself not on a horse, but on a great cat, so swift, deft footed, and serpentine was the twisting course of Moonshine. Clinging as he could, while the shocks numbed his brain and the circling sickened him, he knew that had the mustang possessed a tithe of his ordinary strength, no man could have stayed on his back.

And Moonshine fought with the power of nervous convulsion. He reared and threw back. Lee flung himself clear and rolled away barely in time; the forehoofs of the stallion, as he twisted to his side, missed the face of Lee by a scant fraction of an inch. Lee ran in and scrambled to the back of the horse as Moonshine lurched up again. The rope had been pulled high above his nose—he could not be choked down.

He passed in a frenzy of bucking, straightened out of a dizzy circling, and raced down the valley.

It was incredible that this pitiful skeleton could run with a man on his back, yet run he did, though with a stagger in his gallop. He plunged into a cedar brake and Lee, flattening himself along the back of the mustang, was whipped and cut by the flying branches, but he was still in place when they reached the open. Another scheme came to the horse. He bore to the left and galloped close to the wall of the cliff. A projecting rock edge caught Lee's trousers at the hip and ripped off the leg as cleanly as the bark slides from a willow twig. Providentially it did not reach his flesh, and he hooked his leg in front of the shoulder. But Moonshine now veered from the cliff and halted short with his breath coming like the wind through an old bellows. It was not yet surrender. His head was high, and his ears were pricked as if he had lost all interest in the conflict and was regarding some pleasant form among the clouds. In the pause the hoarse murmur of the waterfall floated up the valley and Lee remembered with a shudder the voice of dead John Ramps.

In that direction the head of the stallion was turned, and as Lee strove to drop the noose lower over the nose of the stallion, Moonshine lunged into a rickety gallop again. Almost at once Lee understood. He knew strange tales of horses who had preferred death to submission. Twice Lee threw his weight back against the rope. It staggered the horse, but did not stop him. He held straight on where the bright rushing of the water dropped into thin air. The voice had grown to a deep, steady chorus.

Still no thought came to Lee of throwing himself from the back of the gray, though he knew that this was no sham charge such as that with which the wise horse had striven to frighten him from the throat of the oxbow loop, on the Rio Grande. For Moonshine, despite rickety gallop and heaving sides, had pricked his ears as though safety lay close before him. To him it was better, far better to die than to yield at the end of the battle, and as the man understood the mind of the horse, he dropped the rope so that it swung wildly from side to side, and, throwing up his hands, he shouted wildly above the rushing of the waters.

A steel-bright curve like the bend of a scimitar, the river dropped over the cliff. Moonshine flung himself into bodiless air. It whirred past the ears of Lee as they fell. He looked up to the blurred blue of the sky. He looked down to the flash of the water beneath them, not in sorrow, but crazy joy, so that the cataract which drowned his senses with noise was like a thunderous burst of music into the heart of which they were hurtling.

He gave a last look to the beautiful, brave head of the horse. Then they struck.

He felt a stinging slap on hands and face. He shot deep into the pool, thrusting farther and farther into the cushioning waters. Still he lived and the rocks had not crushed him! He struck upward and lay on the surface, gasping with a showering of spray in his face. A moment more and he had swum to the shallows, and, standing up in water no deeper than his thighs, he looked about him. The leap he had thought was death was beggarly small. It was not the distance that it fell, but the volume of the river that kept the valley so full of talking echoes.

The stallion was far down the pool, where the current boiled out of the pit, and there the white form whirled in an eddy, lying on its side, and flashing in the sun at each revolution. Lee pushed to the shore and ran stumblingly over the rocks. The eyes of the stallion were closed, the tongue lolled out, and the swift water was carrying away thick streaks of crimson. Plunging into the stream again up to his waist, he caught the head of Moonshine in both his arms, and inch by inch, he drew his prize from the thousand hands of the currents. His heel struck a shelving bank; they were in shoal water, but dizziness began to seize his brain. But, with the help of Providence he would give one last outpouring of his strength! The effort sent the blood out of his head and a wave of darkness began at his feet, sapped the nerves of his knees, and swept up. He felt himself collapsing and struck the air with his open hands as if at an enemy; then, with a last motion of consciousness he caught at and found the head of Moonshine. He sank into black unconsciousness.

9

HALF his body was immersed in the icy water, and this helped to call back his senses. He opened his eyes and found the head of Moonshine lifted above him. Moonshine living! Yes, fiercely alive, for when he rolled away the stallion snapped at him like a wolf. Sitting wearily on the bank Lee watched the struggles of the gray to climb.

They were helpless efforts. Moonshine was trying to drag himself out by one foreleg only, and naturally each effort merely toppled him heavily on the opposite side. Yet he had worked himself high enough to expose the reason why the other foreleg hung idle. The bony outer casing of the hoof was torn loose from the tender flesh and the million nerves within. Exhaustion stopped the stallion. He lay clumsily upon one side, rearing his head up with indomitable courage, and defying the man with great, bright eyes, though his nostrils quivered with pain.

Heavy-limbed, down-headed with exhaustion, Lee studied the case. Here was a wild mustang, willing to die rather than surrender; and, moreover, here was a horse so injured that even the finest doctor might not be able to heal that dreadful wound.

He looked up and down the valley in search of help.

Above them, west and north, ran the line of cliffs over which the river tumbled, but eastward, beginning with the course of the stream, a broad meadow grew up into rolling land and hills behind. Willows straggled along the water edge, and farther back were quaking aspen, cedar, and big firs and spruce as a dark background. Some day it would catch a settler's eye, but at the present there was no hope of succor, and the greatest mercy for the stallion would be quick death. He drew his knife, but looked upward before he opened the blade.

Over the eastern hills great clouds, white and blue and shadowy, came tumbling up into the sky; a bird whistled near him, the world was full of cheer. But in that happy sky he saw half a dozen black specks floating in circles. The buzzards had already marked the fall of the horse. So all the heartbreaking labors of that trail had been to give one more victory to the scavengers. He started to his feet. The hot revolt gave him strength anew, and he hurried down to begin the battle to save Moonshine.

First of all he must give him a dry bed, and since he could not draw the gray from the waters, he must draw the waters from the horse. It was not so very hard to do. He rolled down big stones from the bank and made a wide circle around the stallion. He filled the larger interstices with smaller stones and smooth-edged pebbles. Over the outer surface he next strewed water plants, and, using a section of the outer rind torn from a stump whose heart was pulpy and rotten, he shoveled sand and mud over all the dam until it was watertight. With the same rude shovel he scooped out the water within the dam until at last Moonshine lay on gravel and sand from which the last moisture was swiftly draining away in little rivulets.

He was so exhausted by this time that when he strove to

speak a hearty word to the horse he could only stammer out a thick-throated groan. He must find food at once. In the nearest cedar brake he knocked over a mountain grouse and roasted it hastily. While he ate he could look down through the open woods, to Moonshine by the river. His head had fallen, now, and no doubt he gave himself up for lost. He knew the meaning of the black shapes which circled low and lower from the sky. Perhaps he had seen others of his herd drop in the race and a month later passed the whitening bones. Lee looked again at cliffs, trees, water, and sky, and accepted the chance quietly.

He went down through the meadows where the long, rich grass was growing, and he tore up armfuls of it, as much as he could carry, and brought it back to Moonshine. But the stallion disdained food rank with the man scent. He lifted his head and studied a flight of clouds. But there was endless patience in Lee. He had not been schooled in the long agony of the trail for nothing.

For ten minutes he sat with a tuft of succulent, white-rooted grass presented. And at last, with swift, tentative lips, his eyes fixed guiltily upon the man, Moonshine stole a shred of the grass and gathered it into his mouth, jerking his head high with a snort. He even trembled in fear of the retribution which might overtake him, but the man, in the wealth of his deep and secret wisdom, smiled. He knew how great a victory had just been won.

And to be sure, in a little time, the horse was eating neatly from the palm of his open hand!

The next step in that struggle was far more difficult. It was to bandage the torn hoof, and Lee approached the task with infinite diplomacy. He excavated a small hole on the edge of which he wished to rest the fetlock joint and so suspend the injured hoof where no pressure would grind against the raw nerves. But when the hole was dug, how was he to move that hoof save by bringing his hand within reach of teeth that might crush the bones to a pulp? But even that terrible risk he was willing to take. He advanced, little by little, the hand from which the horse had eaten, and all the while his steady voice brought a thousand glittering lights playing and softening in the eyes of the stallion. When, at length, his fingers touched the slender leg, the gray head darted down like a striking snake, and the teeth fastened over Lee's forearm.

But they did not close. He released the arm as suddenly as he had seized it, and, raising his head, he looked far off at the flashing of the sun on a young poplar. It was almost as though he were ashamed. But when Lee raised the leg gently and placed the fetlock joint on the edge of the hole, the relief from pain was so instant that Moonshine lowered his head again and snuffed at the merciful hand of the man with trembling nostrils.

The worst part of caring for the hoof was no doubt passed when Moonshine submitted to his touch. He went on with more assurance. With his clumsy shovel he drove a trench from above his own dam and led down a clear, sparkling rivulet which he enlarged to a pool just in front of Moonshine.

The washing alone filled the hour until sunset. It was work which brought out a perspiration of sympathy on Lee. He had to pry the loose shell away from the sensitive laminae and then pour into the opening cold water. It was like flooding the naked nerve of a gigantic tooth, but though the horse dropped his head, and the muscle of his foreleg kept jumping, he did not stir his foot.

After the cleansing ended, Lee delicately but firmly pressed the hoof shell into place and bound it with supple willow bark. Around this he packed thick layers of the cooling clay, laid splints of fir over the clay to keep the hoof rigidly in place, and covered the whole with withes of creeping vines and another wet layer of mud. That done, he must leave the rest to time and chance.

A time of hard work began. Moonshine ate voraciously, and every mouthful had to be carried from the meadow far away where he tore up the grass. There was his necessary bedding, also, for he could not lie continually on the bruising gravel. All this was in a broken season of rain, wind, and sun of alternate fierceness, so he built Moonshine a shelter. First he felled saplings with circles of fire and then fixed them up deep in the earth around the horse. When he bent their heads and tied them together with creepers he had the frame of a wikiup upon which he laid a thatching.

For his own food he skirmished with stones or stick for the clumsy, sleepy grouse or laid deadfalls for the birds where their established paths wound through the grass, baiting the traps with dried seed. Best of all he invented fishhooks whittled out of wing bones, and with these and a strong creeper, or a strand of the rope, he fished successfully in the river a half mile below.

He could not make these excursions long, however, for there was never a day when he did not hear or see evidences of mountain lion or wolf prowling near and waiting for their prey. Moreover, a long absence sent the horse into a frenzy of neighing. Even when Lee was in the meadow plucking the grass he would wait for the stallion's neigh and then answer with a high, wailing whistle that pierced through the heaviest wind.

It was strange how swiftly and joyously the days drifted by while he waited for the time when Moonshine could be safely helped to his feet. He himself was greatly changed.

Sometimes when he fished, leaning over still water, he saw himself masked in a savage beard with hair straggling down his shoulders. He was naked to the waist, and below the waist his ragged trousers did not reach his knees. His feet had been bare for many days, and the soles were horny as leather. But with hardships came perfect freedom with only one shadow clouding his mind, and that was the great question of Moonshine's hoof. When he removed the bandage he might find only a ragged, shriveled parody of a hoof. When he thought of that he could not help looking into the sky where the buzzards still hung. His patience was great, but theirs was endless.

It became increasingly difficult after the first few days to keep Moonshine quiet. He gained in strength and flesh with amazing rapidity, and, with the addition of vigor, he waxed more eager to find his feet. After that it was necessary to pet and amuse the stallion like a sick child until Lee decided that he might safely get up.

To insure that safety, however, was a great problem, for Moonshine must get to his feet without once putting an ounce of weight upon the injured hoof. To prevent that, Lee made of tough vines a sling which passed over the withers, fastened at the elbow, and again, firmly, around the fetlock joint, which was drawn close to the upper leg. He now began a course of lessons, teaching Moonshine to rise on one foreleg, throwing part of his weight upon the shoulder of the man. It was prodigious hard labor for the cow-puncher to take that great forward thrust as the mustang lunged up, but it was finally accomplished. Moonshine came swaying to his feet and hobbled out of the wikiup with Lee at his side, supporting all he could of the weight. The horse stayed up only a short time the first day; before he became unsteady on his three feet Lee had to maneuver him back into the wikiup.

Inside it Moonshine turned around like a dog in his kennel, found the exact old spot, and lowered himself cautiously into it. It was a triumph for both of them, and Lee spent an hour foolishly gathering the seeded heads of grasses, a work which Moonshine devoured in two or three careless mouthfuls.

Still the end was far away, and if the hurt hoof were exposed and used a single day too soon, all their weeks of effort would be spent in vain. He examined it with painful interest each time he changed the dressing, and always the hoof looked worse, for while the other three were worn down nearly to normal as Moonshine hobbled around on them day after day, the bandaged foot grew steadily and became a disproportioned, hideous thing, with a great hard rim where the wound was knitting. But Lee knew that his eye could not tell him. Not until Moonshine put his weight on that foot and limped or walked straight would he know.

10

ON top of a hill which was burned brown by the full heat of summer stood Moonshine, a bright form against the blue sky beyond him. He went readily on three legs, now, hobbling everywhere, and even managing occasionally a broken canter. Each day he roamed farther, and Lee, marking this journey to the distant hill, mused somberly over it. For all those excursions were toward the north. "He's turning back to his kin," Lee decided. "Hoof and hide and hair, every inch of him wants to be back there with his wild devils." What made the conclusion doubly important was that this day he had determined to cut the sling and let the injured hoof strike the ground. He raised that keen whistle, and the mustang swung about with a whinny and came at the hobbling canter down the slope to him.

"Old hoss," the man said, "this is your day. Either you're as free as the clouds, blowing yonder, or else you'll be fodder for them."

He lifted the chin of the stallion and made him look up where the buzzards hung, waiting. Then he ripped away the covering of withes and clay and last and cut the sling at the withers. Down came the foot, but as it struck the earth Moonshine heeled over and barely saved a fall by lurching off on three feet with the lame hoof raised high. Lee Garrison closed his eyes.

"Buzzard food—him!" whispered the cow-puncher. And with his eyes still closed, he groaned: "Moonshine!"

Moonshine came at a trot and Lee listened sadly for the bobbling break in the rhythm. But true and clear the rhythm of that trot was beat. He opened his eyes. It was true; the injured hoof was striking the ground in its turn—gingerly, to be sure, but regularly.

"Run, damn you!"

Moonshine threw himself about and stretched across the meadow at a gallop—a limping gallop, but a true one, with healed foot pounding in its turn. Halting, he looked back with ears pointed in suspicion, as if he had seen a new creature jump out of the form of his companion. But Lee neither stirred nor shouted; joy had closed his throat.

They did not leave the old camp even then, but day by day they roamed through the hills together until the weak leg grew strong, and the long muscles were once more worn down to the shape of its fellows, with only the disappearing ridge to mark the wound. Then he broke camp. He threw away even the rope, for if it came to a battle he could never ride this revivified stallion. He felt it as he stood, on this morning, beside the stallion, with his hand on the withers. Once before he had been on that back, but in those days it had been a ridge of bone, and now that hollow was filled with rounding, smooth muscles.

"Moonshine," he said.

The stallion turned his head.

"This part was never wrote into the contract, old fellow," said Lee, "but the straight of it is that I figure on using your feet as much as you use 'em. Which you still got the right to have your say and dump me on my head; no hard feeling if you do—but here goes!"

He swung back, made a quick step forward, and vaulted onto the back of Moonshine. There, with his hand buried in the mane, and his knees feeling for a firmer hold, he waited while the strong body under him quivered, settled. He set his teeth for the leap straight into the air, but instead, Moonshine sprang into a gallop as smooth as the run of an ocean wave. Or, freer still, it was as though wings buoyed him and shot him forward with wind whipping his face. A hill drifted past them, a valley was devoured by those flying hoofs, and still the flight was not abated. They shot over a hill. Below, a long slope tumbled east toward the red of the dawn, and the gray flung himself out with head lowering. Like the rush of water down smooth rock, they shot into the heart of the morning. To try to stop him now would be like trying to recall a loosed arrow. Yet Lee stooped till the tips of the mane were snapping his face and called softly. Behold! The head went up, the run checked to a swinging canter. The arrow had heeded the voice!

But Lee Garrison learned, in the days that followed, that no matter how easily the horse could be swung from side to side or halted, he continually swung back toward the north as a boat struggles to come before the wind. At last, feeling that the test must come sooner or later, he let Moonshine follow his own will, and before sunset of a still hot day, they came over a hill and saw wild horses in the hollow beneath.

The herd was not caught unawares. Already the outposts had brought in the warning of a man's approach, and now a fine chestnut stallion was whipping in the laggards, grouping his herd together. Finally with a neigh he started them away at full gallop. Moonshine tore off in pursuit. Lee drew back on the mane and shouted. The pace of the silver-gray shortened, not to the rolling canter, but to a gait like a choppy sea. He called again, and the stallion reared and stopped, but with head strained high he stared at the fleeing herd. Was this his own band? Lee slid to the ground. Still with the weight of two fingers on that arched neck he held the horse.

"Moonshine, there's one thing," he said, "that time ain't going to change. Your kind ain't my kind. Here I am, and there run your horses. Make your choice."

There was not even a turn of Moonshine's head in answer. When the fingers lifted he was off with one high sway of his tail, and a neigh that rang across the hill ridges and to the herd. Some of them, as if they recognized the command, shortened their gallop. There no longer remained much doubt that they were recognizing the old leader. Indeed in a few more moments the whole crowd had slowed to a trot and the chestnut came swinging back to investigate. Moonshine went down the hill to meet him.

It was a beautiful thing to see the two come together, falling from gallop to canter, from canter to trot, from trot to nervous, high-stepping walk. Behind them the herd scattered into a semicircle, the wise old mare in the rear calling to the yearlings to keep them back, and restless young stallions coming curiously forward to watch and get points from the two champions. Nose to nose they met, arching neck. The pricked ears snapped suddenly back. With a squeal of rage the chestnut plunged at the throat of Moonshine with gaping teeth.

A spring to one side, as if the wind had blown him, took the gray out of danger, and the new leader, floundering at the end of his rush, whirled and charged again while Moonshine watched with his head canted thoughtfully to one side. But he was ready for blood now. Up he reared and rained blows at the chestnut's snaky head. The new leader gave back with sinking hindquarters, dazed, but he had the bulldog blood which runs in all mustangs. He charged again, and this time he, also, reared. Apparently that was the opening for which the gray had hopes, as the old pugilist waits to shoot his favorite blow. He sprang forward with a short whinny—like a snarl, almost drove through the barrage of the striking forehoofs, and caught the new leader by the throat. The new leader went down, and Lee covered his eyes to shut away the rest of the horrible picture as Moonshine charged over the fallen horse.

A moment later there was a great neigh and a beat of hoofs running toward him. It was Moonshine, his bright coat spotted with red. He swept about Lee in a spiral which ended when, with all fours planted, he slid to a halt. His muscle was red and his eyes were devilish. Behind him, down the slope, was the shapeless blotch which had been the chestnut leader. Lee neither moved nor spoke.

Moonshine danced away, sidewise, like a boxer, and at the little distance he whinnied. It was clear to Lee, at last, that he was invited to join the herd, but still, though his heart was thundering, he would neither move nor use the persuasion of his voice. He found a sullen, tormented pleasure in leaving the choice to the horse.

The herd no longer waited, but moved down the valley at a trot, and at the head ran a fine bay—a new aspirant for the vacancy. When Moonshine neighed the ranks wavered and spread, but the bay called in turn, and they went on. Off went Moonshine down the slope, but halfway to the herd he whirled as suddenly as he had started, and, looking back, he neighed and stamped in a fretful fury of impatience. Another feint of going on with the herd brought no movement from Lee, so at last Moonshine came slowly up the hill, plodding with head fallen.

By Lee he stopped and turned, and, together, they watched the wild horses drop over a ridge.

11

THE upper Samson Mountains crowded together behind them as Lee Garrison rode Moonshine into the southern range, bound for the staked plains. It was a long trail, but over every mile that he had labored on foot he would now gallop on the back of the stallion. Indeed, he almost wished that the trail would never end; on such a horse he felt that he should go on to some glorious destiny. What bright goal was possible to a cow-puncher? Like a child on a feast day, shutting out the thought of tomorrow and its school, he lost himself in delight of the moment.

They came out, on a day, to the shoulder of a hill, the arm of which had been chopped off; they came at a swinging gallop, and Moonshine slid to a halt, knocking up a shower of pebbles which dropped silently out of sight beyond the edge. A more clumsy animal might have plunged with its rider where those stones were falling, but so accustomed had

Lee grown to the goat-footed surety of his horse that he merely laughed at the dizzy thought and let Moonshine step still nearer to the verge until they could look down between the hollow walls of the cañon to its floor.

At this season the stream which had ploughed the gorge among the mountains was a muddy trickle among big sun-whitened rocks which its spring current would roll again toward the sea. At the head of the little valley there was a hundred-foot cliff above the broad scar of the waterfall where now only a few streaks glistened on the flat rock face. Close to it was the first house he had seen in all the hunt from the southland, and now his heart fell at the sight of it!

Here ended his holiday. The world from which he had run away returned to him. He could not play forever. Inescapable duty called to him. Duty to what? He was answerable to no man. Yet the heavy truth oppressed him; there was something he must do! It bewildered him; and the harder he grasped at an understanding, the more completely it evaded him. There could be nothing less imposing than yonder little wedge of a roof, unpainted and melting into the weathered brown of the cliff, but yonder little house sheltered one of those outliers of civilization, one of those hardy fellows who tear a livelihood out of rocks and sand. The very thought of his labor cast a burden of weariness upon Lee. He wrinkled his forehead; there was an ache in his heart. For tomorrow he must go and do likewise.

He groaned at last so that Moonshine, who with wise head canted had been studying the descent into the valley, now pricked his ears suddenly and turned with eloquent question to watch the master. So brave was that lifted head that Lee was shamed for his falling of the heart, and though instinct warned him to shut this cañon and its house from sight and mind, yet a perverse impulse forced him on. He loosed the reins, but having learned long before that Moonshine's unguided way was generally the best in mountain work, he made no effort to pick a course. The gray, accordingly, after considering his task with another glance, started to the side. Thirty seconds of plunging, sliding, and leaping like a mountain sheep, and they came out smoothly upon the cañon floor. There the rider looked back at the course where they had slid, like water down the rock, and with that past danger exhilarating him he turned with a laugh toward the house. Yonder fellow should pay for these pains with a cup of coffee, at least.

But now that he was close he saw that the shack was unoccupied. He dropped the saddle and stepped toward it with Moonshine, doglike, at his heels. Under the pressure of his hand the door gave way from the rust-eaten hinges and crashed in, sending a heavy ripple of dust across the floor. It was obviously intended as a summer house only, no doubt for use through a single season. How old it was he could not guess, for one winter might have rotted these flimsy boards, and the interior was in hopeless confusion owing to the fall of a boulder from the cliff above. It had carried the major portion of the roof with it in its fall, and now arose in the exact center of the floor, littered over with the ruin of its own making. On the whole, it was as dreary a bit of spoiled carpentry as one could hope to find, but Garrison looked about him with painful interest. The collapsing shack was a sharp reminder that beyond the foothills lay a world which claimed him, to which he must return, in which he must accomplish a man's work. A sense of truancy made Garrison as hollow of heart as the small boy when he hears the school bells, chiding.

He began to kick at the loose planks, grumbling so that Moonshine came halfway through the door and set up a tremendous din pawing to find out what was the matter, until the first word Lee had ever spoken to him in a harsh voice reduced the horse to a high-headed silence. Lee continued to explore. In one corner a cheap little cast-iron stove sagged toward the floor. Beside the window hung a strip of what had once been a curtain, of a weather-faded pink. A bit of yellow paper fluttered in the corner, and he picked it up. He could make out the accurate delicacy of a girl's handwriting, but the ink was too blurred for reading. A moment later he kicked away a section of the fallen roof and found beneath it a glove, uncrushed. Garrison picked it up. It was a woman's glove, for the right hand, and made of tanned kid. The frayed tips told why it had been abandoned. The leather was femininely soft as he drew at the glove aimlessly and squeezed three fingers into the palm. At this a foolish thrill brought him out of his daydream. He hurried over to the corner and found the bit of paper once more. It was the beginning of an unfinished letter, and it proved that she who lived in this cabin, who wore this glove, who wrote this letter, was young. If she were young, might she not be beautiful? Yes, a sweet and startling surety came to him as though her bright ghost whispered from a corner. But where, where was she now? He brushed past Moonshine into the open.

Below him in curling range on range the hills poured down to the plain. Men lived there; men labored there; wedded in yonder blue distance.

A soft nose touched his shoulder. Guiltily he began to caress the stallion, but at length his hand fell away and he found himself staring once more into the horizon. So he folded the glove and stowed it in his hip pocket with a frown.

"Why, Moonshine," he said. "I've been cussing out the world without remembering that I don't know a thing about

77

it. I've never known a man, really. I've sure never known a woman. Mountains are all well enough. But they can't talk to you. They can't smile at you. Why, partner, you and me have got a lot to find out about. Let's start the trail!"

If Moonshine did not fathom the peroration he at least understood the act which followed it, consisting of a leap onto his back and a touch of heels on his flank. He was down the valley with a toss of the tail and a lift of the head.

Until the dusk they traveled south over the hills, but in the first soft falling of the dark Lee made for a camp fire that twinkled in the distance and then shone out like a huge yellow star. The star grew into a leaping fire, with a man moving in black silhouette on one side and a pack mule cropping dead bunch grass on the other.

Moonshine began to dance in anxiety, and Lee, to encourage him, dropped to the ground and walked on ahead. His own heart was warm long before he came into the heat of the fire, it was so marvelously good to see a human being again! As he came into the circle of the fire light he called out a greeting, and the camper whirled with an exclamation. The sight of him stole half of Lee's joy for such a starving bit of manhood he had never seen before. He was perhaps an inch or so over five feet, and so thin that even under heavy cloth one was constantly aware of hunched shoulders, elbows, and knees. So shrunken was his flesh that one could see the death's head through his features.

His greeting for the newcomer was a shrill cry and a reaching for a gun. Indeed, the appearance of Lee was by no means reassuring. His long hair was blown forward about a face covered with ragged beard; he was more than half naked; and he was attended close at heels by a gray horse out of a dream, which was ridden, apparently, without reins.

Moreover, this fellow was brown as an Indian, and his eyes by the fire light seemed wild and bright as the eyes of the horse.

The pistol wobbled in the shaking hand of the little man, while he cried: "Keep off, chief! I need plenty of room, understand? Don't crowd me, because if you try to jump this gun, you'll finish off. Heap plenty room, chief, understand?"

The big gun in the unpracticed hand set Lee trembling, but though he pushed his hands above his shoulders he could not help smiling at the stranger's fear of "Indians."

He explained amiably that he was a cow-puncher, not a redskin wanderer, and briefly told how he had trailed Moonshine and worn him down at the expense of months of labor. Perhaps his smile was the only necessary part of his explanation. The first mention of the horse was the concluding touch, for the little man forgot about his gun and stepped closer to Moonshine. The stallion crowded up to the back of Lee in fear, snorting and stamping while the man of the camp fire moved about him.

"Nice show horse," said the little stranger at length, nodding his head, "and he'd do for a lady's saddle work, I guess. But what he needs is legs. That's what a horse runs with; how can he get along without 'em?"

"Get along?" cried Lee, "why, man, this is Moonshine! Get along? He can get along all day and—"

The other raised his hand. "What can he do six furlongs in?" he asked. "Suppose I was to try to work him a mile in forty-five? Why, he simply couldn't stretch it, that's all! I could fan dust in his face with a five-year-old maiden that never limped a half in fifty-two! You walked a thousand miles for—that?"

Lee was blind with anger, but the usefulness of the man

tied his hands. The little man took the silence for surrender, and he continued more kindly. "But I always say that a man's horse is like a wife, you can't judge him by what he plays. I seen old Sure-shot Billy himself drop ten thousand on a three-legged filly, Mischief, to beat Kitty Bellairs, herself. I seen Sure-shot lay that wad myself. 'Billy,' says I, 'if you want to get rid of some money, for heaven's sake remember your friends and let the bookies go.'"

He laughed prodigiously at his story, his laughter sounding like the crowing of a rooster, and when Lee chuckled at him it did not occur to the man at the camp fire that he was the jest rather than the jester. His heart was so warmed that a few moments later Moonshine had eaten his first grains of barley from the hand of Lee, and Lee himself was supping on the fare of Buddy Slocum.

The withered little man was so glad of company, so full of talk, that he gave Lee no time to answer an opening volume of questions, but followed at once with an account of himself. He was an ex-jockey who, having made a few thousand dollars by a lucky coup on a long shot, had read at the same time an obscure account of the strike at Crooked Creek, and had resolved that while his lucky spell was on him he would go West to dig gold from the ground instead of out of the pockets of the bookmakers. It was a sad decision, said Buddy Slocum. Everything had gone wrong from the first. Finally he had reached a town within striking distance of the mines and had crowned the follies of his expedition by buying a pack and pack mule and going off among the hills. Of course he had lost his way, and after rambling four days, a horseman, bound for Crooked Creek, had passed him and directed him again. Now the mines were only a short distance south, and they were marked by a mountain near by whose summit glittered with an outcropping of white rock, visible afar. In the meantime, his stock of money was shrunk from several thousands to hardly as many hundreds. However, now the mines were not far off. Before the week was out, who could tell? He might be rich and already started back for Broadway!

To this tale, which lasted until the tins had been washed after the meal, Lee Garrison listened with a growing dissatisfaction. This ugly hard-eyed cheat began to seem typical of the entire race of men to which he was returning. He only saved himself from heavy melancholy by concentrating on the speech of the ex-jockey and trying to forget the speaker. The name of the mines gave him a chilly sense of the length of time he had been away from the world. Before he started on the trail of Moonshine, many weeks before, there had been no word in the West of such a place as Crooked Creek. Buddy Slocum now reached a stopping point and proposed a game of stud poker.

"I been playing solitaire," said he, "and that's like Christmas without turkey."

Lee refused; he had no money.

"Stake a share in Moonshine," pleaded Buddy. "We'll start as small as you like," urged the man of the race track. "There's a rope on the gray that's worth a dollar. Put that up. You'll have poor man's luck."

It was true prophecy. He could not lose. That last of the deal, that fluttering fifth card which decided one's fate in stud, was always a lucky card for Lee. In five minutes his dollar was twenty, and Slocum promptly raised the stakes with a sigh of satisfaction as he saw the game take on some semblance of real earnest. His new energy, however, brought him no better fortune. His losing was now a fixed habit. From twenty to a hundred was a quick step for Lee. From one hundred his winnings rose to two while the manner of Buddy Slocum gradually changed from careless assurance to a cold and sneering intentness.

"Beginner's luck," suggested Lee.

"Beginner's luck?" echoed the other with emphasis. "Beginner's luck? I guess not, Garrison. But go on with the game. I ain't howling. First time I've been the fall guy in quite a while. Keep right on trying, pal!"

Just what Slocum meant, Lee could not understand for a time, but it was easy to see that the ex-jockey was in a silent temper. A few minutes later Lee won a fat bet with four little sevens over three jacks and a pair of aces, and Slocum rose to his feet.

"I'm through," he said. "I've got fifty left, and I'll keep it for luck."

Lee dragged the entire quantity of his winnings from his pockets. It was more cash than he had ever seen before. The bills were fives and tens and now he crunched scores of them under his fingers. One escaped and tumbled away across the tarpaulin on which they had been playing. Buddy Slocum's foot stirred, but he resisted the impulse and let the green-back roll past.

"I can't start with a rope end and get all this," said Lee frankly. "Besides, I was playing for fun, not for the coin. Take it back, Slocum. You're mighty welcome to it."

This brought a snarl from Slocum, a veritable animal whine of rage. Instantly he was in a trembling, panting fury. He was no cheap sport, no yellow four-flusher he declared. But from the very first he had suspected that Lee was crooking the deal. Now he knew it. But let it go. The world was a small place. They would meet again, and then let Lee beware! In the meantime the mountains offered plenty of room for them both, and he invited Lee to start for new quarters.

Lee started, of course, and that night he was for long unable to sleep when he finally found grass for the gray and shelter for himself under the lee of a hill. Shame and disgust, as he reviewed the scene with Buddy Slocum, kept him awake, turning from side to side and gritting his teeth. This, then, was a foretaste of what he was to expect in the society of his fellows?

Here he drew out the glove and ran the soft leather through his fingers. The strange-hearted hope rose again, and with it the feeling between sorrow and laughter. After all, there was a rustle and crisping of money in his pocket, and that meant feathering for his arrow that would carry him far in the pursuit.

He began to try to visualize her face. Before he succeeded, he was asleep.

12

It was noon before Moonshine topped the northern ridge overlooking Crooked Creek. Darting back and forth among the boulders, a tan-colored stream, frothy here and there with the speed of its going, Crooked Creek had torn for itself a sharp-lipped cañon.

From ridge to ridge the gulch had been hewn through solid rhyolite. How many thousands of drillers, how many tons of dynamite would have been needed to duplicate that excavation? Lee wrinkled his brow. There was pain of labor even in the thought. But the beauty of that rock! Wherever erosion had trenched away the stone was pigment unrusted and undimmed. Weathering could not tarnish that pale straw yellow or canary tinted with green. There was a lilac mist, streaked through and through with heavy cardinal, and yonder a lavender haze with chalk-white strata above it. And all these colors in solid rock! To Lee it seemed rather a bank of fog pierced with sunset colors, living with beauty.

But between him and the creek the soft and mingling hues of the rhyolite were cut athwart by a fish-fin ridge of dirty yellow porphyry. Two miles up and down the gorge it ran with the mines distributed about it; forty or fifty dumps Lee estimated, and over each was a gallows frame for the whip or upright for the windlass, and every stick of these timbers painted dark red. As if color were needed in Crooked Creek!

There were myriad noises afloat in the gulch where a hundred double jacks rang on the drill heads, where men were shouting, where windlasses squeaked and the horse-turned drums were groaning. Moreover, all these voices struck through the rarefied mountain air. But though cables shrieked and hammers rang, the desert silence was more powerful than all the uproar. From the opposite cliffs, echo melted ten voices together and flung them across the valley tenfold magnified. Yet the mountain quiet cradles the noise into harmonies. Half a mile away a miner was shooting eight ringing blasts, but they blew to the ear of Lee like eight notes of music.

But the mines themselves were of the least importance to Lee. It was the town he wished to see, and what a town it was! It ran the full length of the gulch, not more than a stone's throw in breadth at any point, but two miles long, an amazing huddle of tent tops and roofs, given a living shape by the sinuous twisting of the river. Below the town the hills fell away at once to the flat; the rock-tearing river became a placid little stream, and by its left bank a road wound away into the lowlands.

It was an amazingly busy thoroughfare over the naked plain. The air was so thin, so dry that distance reduced objects in size, but did not blur them. Five little wagons, each drawn by six or eight Lilliputian nags, pushed up the slope. The dust clouds rose and melted away. He felt the labor of the team, nodding in rhythm; it seemed surprising that he could not hear the creaking of singletree and wagon bed. Farther off some riders, singly, or in groups, and another caravan was working out of the blue horizon. Another sound of blasting struck up the slope at him like a giant shouting to the world in a great, thick accent; gold!

With joy in his throat he sent Moonshine down the slope. He wanted to sing, to shout, for under the morning shadow which was sinking in the gulley was power which could be dug out of the earth and held in his hands—gold! That great magician could find him the lady of the glove and make the road to her only a step. Moonshine swayed on a perilous course among the boulders, but Lee Garrison had raised his face to the glove which he flaunted on high, and she whose hand had once filled it was now so clear, so smilingly near, that he could almost see the gleam of her eyes at the end of this trail. She had been etched in his brain before with delicate touches, pale as a vapor in moonlight, but now she was just around the corner from his hope.

He dropped into an increasing uproar in the heart of the valley. It seemed that so many men breaking ground must surely sink a way to the very roots of the hills. In the meantime he had no opportunity to look about, for Moonshine was dancing like a cat on wet ground or crouched with shuddering fear under a sudden weight of racket. With soothing hand and voice Lee kept him on the trembling verge of panic, but it was growing doubly difficult. Men began to tumble out of the mines and came to watch the passing of the half-naked brown man on the white stallion. Never were such men as these miners, so huge, so grimy, their faces besmudged with a stubble of beard. They came, some of them, with the eight-pound hammer still weighing down their hands. Every face was a new dread to Moonshine. He went along with tensed, catlike steps, and now and again, pausing an instant, he jerked up his head and looked with wild eyes toward the blessed peace of the mountains. Yet he did not bolt, not even when the miners laughed and pointed at the rider.

As for Lee, he accepted that laughter with an ease which was amazing to himself.

It had been so long since he had seen men—except the ratlike countenance of Buddy Slocum—that he overflowed with good nature. In the other days he would have been tortured with shame to be made such a public show, but men who are starved forget fear, and Lee was famine struck with need of human society. He laughed back at the crowd and waved a brown arm to them. Then some one in the background shouted: "Moonshine!" It was a fellow with a face pinched up into the shadow of a vast sombrero. "I've seen him with binoculars. I've seen him as clear as a picture. It's the Moonshine hoss."

A whisper, washed out from that speaker, spread up the slope on either side, and from the distance where the double jacks were beating, new voices shouted, other men came running. A solid wall of the curious men closed across Lee's path. He stopped the terrified gray.

"He ain't trained to stand for his picture, yet. Let me through, boys," called Lee. "It's Moonshine, right enough."

What admiration and wonder shone in their eyes! They gaped up at him like children, and a path split through the crowd. They volleyed their questions as he rode through.

How had he captured the famous horse? What wild work had given him the semblance of a red Indian? How long had he been on the trail? Would he stay in Crooked Creek? There was not time to answer. Many went back to their work with a shouted promise to see him again. But a round dozen remained to escort him in triumph. The dozen in that escort became five hundred by the time they had passed half a block up the dusty, rutted street of Crooked Creek, for if there were fifteen thousand in that strange city, fourteen thousand five hundred had no better occupation than to rush from point to point to hear or see the latest sensation. All that Lee saw, in his first intimate glimpse of the mining town, was an acre of upturned, grinning faces.

He was asked where he wanted to go, and when he said his first need was a bunk for himself and a place for the horse, they brought him to a flat-roofed shack. They waited until the door was opened by a little gray-haired woman in blue gingham which shone with starch and ironing. She threw up her hands with a cry at sight of a wild man riding a horse without saddle or bridle, and the gesture made Moonshine whirl and leap away. The crowd scattered with a yell of pleasure to see the bucking, but they were deeply disappointed, for when Lee slipped to the ground and approached the door on foot, Moonshine crowded against his heels, throwing his head high so that he could keep in view all the terrible strangers who stood behind him.

In a moment the agreement was made. Mrs. Samuels, the landlady of the lodging house, led the way to the rear where a little corral had been fenced with smooth wire. Her son had built it for his horse, she explained, but her son's horse could be tethered on the outside. So the gray stallion was led through the gate and Lee closed it upon him. Moonshine bounded to the center, and then veered swiftly around the enclosure. He halted at last in terror, and Lee turned away sadly, for he knew that this was the end of their free companionship and the beginning of slavery for Moonshine.

He was shown by Mrs. Samuels to her only vacant room. The price was three dollars for eight hours; and Lee, flushed with gambler's luck, took all three shifts for himself. The room was exactly six by eight. It was partitioned from the hall by one canvas sheet, and separated from the adjoining room by another. The furniture was a cheap folding cot and a chair, constructed from a box. The distinguishing feature was that the canvas flap, which served as a window, opened upon the street.

"The view would be pretty fine?" suggested Mrs. Samuels, cocking her head to one side as she smiled up to him. "You wouldn't be getting lonely in a room like that, now!"

One could not choose in Crooked Creek. She assured him it was the only available room in the town, so he paid his rent and went out to find clothes and a barber. In five minutes a hoarse-voiced, weary man in the store outfitted him with clothes, shoes, hat, cartridge belt, a revolver. In the corner of the store he threw off his old rags and stepped into his new costume. By the grace of chance it fitted him, fitted far too closely for the comfort of one grown accustomed to well-nigh skin-free abandon. The groaning tightness of the boots, the heat and weight of the clothes made Lee remember Moonshine and the encircling turn of the fence. Truly there was a burden in civilization! But somewhere in the background of noises in that busy little town a woman was singing an indistinguishable air. Perhaps it was she whose glove now rested in his breast pocket, for since Moonshine had become his horse, all miracles were possible! He started eagerly on the trail of a barber.

In such a camp one might have expected a barber to be a superfluous luxury, but luxuries outspeed many a necessity on the road to a gold-rush town; there may be a vital shortage of canned beans, but there are sure to be diamonds. Lee found the barber in a shop made expeditiously by leaning a few planks against the side of a building. He sat down on a box to wait while the barber finished with another patron. They chatted busily the while.

The barber was a stodgy man. His face ran down from a meager forehead into jowls that drooped loosely over his collar; his body sloped out from narrow shoulders to a great girth of abdomen. His lips were generally parted, and the lower one thrust out a little. In addition he had a habit of panting between phrases and motions. In spite of these handicaps he was managing to do business in two ways with his customer. While he removed the hair from the face of the man, he struck terms for grubstaking the latter.

"The last one started like a beauty and then pinched out on me," declared the one who was being shaved. "I was in bonanza for a day, and after that I was nowhere. You're sure white for fixing me up for a new start, Gus, but you'll get back a thousand percent. I know the place; I know the place for it!"

He started clapping his hands on his knees and could hardly remain for the shaving to be finished, such was his eagerness to start out anew with pack and burro. When he left he poured out one burst of frantic gratitude. The barber cut him short by thrusting a slip of paper into his hand.

"You go to Swinnerton over in the store," he said. "He'll give you what you want when he sees that. Now run along. And—"

He was interrupted by a crash of hoofbeats in the street and then a roar of voices that acted on the receiver of the grubstake like the reaching of an invisible hand. He lurched from the entrance and sped out of sight.

"Somebody's made a big strike," interpreted the barber,

motioning Lee into the chair and then running a comb with affectionate dexterity through the long masses of hair. "Somebody's made a big strike, and somebody else has grabbed the news and come in to spill it. What you want? All this taken off?"

"A clean shave and a short cut," answered Lee. "But how come you can stay in here shaving people and grubstaking 'em when they're scooping the gold up in buckets at Crooked Creek?"

Gus lifted a handful of the locks and shore them away with a grinding slash of the scissors.

"I'll get a handful out of some of them scoops," he said. "I'll get a little if my luck lasts. Sure to if I run into many like that Bill White that just went out."

"Good miner, eh? Known him a long time?"

"About half an hour! Yes, he's a good miner."

"Half an hour!" exclaimed Lee. "And yet you grubstake him?"

"I've grubstaked some, five minutes after I met 'em. I'd rather know 'em short than long."

"Well," murmured Lee sympathetically, "I hope you don't lose your money."

"But you think I will, eh? Look here, son, if you got eyes to read with, you can see what's on a page in a couple of seconds, can't you? Same way, you can see what's in a man, if you know the language he's wrote in." He grunted complacently.

"You mean to say you look right through gents, maybe?" suggested Lee. "You can tell what he's going to do? What luck he'll have?"

"No place better than a barber's chair for reading a man," said the other. "I been working the camps close onto thirty years, and I've always worked 'em with a razor." He

90

elaborated on his jest, chuckling. "Dig my gold with a razor—does a cleaner job!"

"You generally win out?"

"One in five pays me back; one in ten makes some money for me; one in a hundred hit it big. That's good enough for me. No, son, a barber's chair is my gold mine. See right through a gent when he's got soap on his face. Maybe that's because they got such a foolish look when they roll their eyes up at you."

Lee smiled in his turn, for with the hair cutting accomplished, Gus was now working up the lather, walking back and forth from the chair to the little stove on which the hot water steamed.

"Well," said Lee, after he had puffed the soap from his lips, "what chance would I have of getting a grubstake?"

The barber stepped back a little, poising his razor and thrusting out his lower lip. But in a moment he was smiling. When he smiled his face was more froglike than ever. He continued the shaving.

"Well?" asked Lee.

"Tut, tut," chuckled the barber. "You ain't a digger, son. You're a spender. You ain't a digger, and why should I give money to a spender?"

"You don't figure me to be very thrifty, eh?"

"Look here," growlingly replied Gus, his good humor vanishing as distinctly as a snap of the fingers, and as suddenly. "Look here, I ain't a fortune-teller; I'm a barber. I get paid for taking the hair off a gent's face, not for reading his palm. That's the trouble with all you youngsters. So plumb wrapped up in yourselves it tickles you right to the gizzard to have folks talk about you. Well, I'd rather talk about the weather!"

He continued to mutter to himself and Lee, abashed,

attempted an expression of stern dignity, sadly marred when the barber slapped the skin taut on one side of his face for a polishing stroke. At least, his fee was most moderate, when he had finished.

"Well," he said, as his customer rose, "you don't look near so big, now that you got your whiskers off. Maybe you don't feel so big, either. Whiskers are queer things. They fool the gent that wears 'em more than the other folks that see 'em. I got two boys, one as much like the other as two peas in a pod; both great talkers. Jerry trimmed his mustaches off short and fashionable and darned if he didn't get to be a traveling salesman and talks as smooth as you please. And Joe let his mustaches grow long at the ends and hang down, and so he had to go in for politics. Jerry saves dollars out of his talking and Joe saves newspaper clippings. Jerry says he'll sell twice as much when he can afford to buy a diamond stickpin as big as his thumb nail, and Joe is chewing his lip and waiting to get bald. He says a bald head is his ticket to Washington. You see what a difference it made to them kids, the ways they grew their mustaches?"

Lee Garrison, listening and smiling in spite of himself, stroked his skin as though it were a newly acquired property.

"Partner," he said suddenly, "I guess you're all right. Maybe I did feel a little big."

The barber nodded amiably, for nothing so softens the heart as criticism accepted. He even followed Lee to the entrance, and added: "And if I was you, son, I'd slip off that gun belt and gun and drop it private in a place where you wouldn't find it in a hurry. Maybe you can use it well enough not to have to do any shooting, but the sheriff ain't very active in Crooked Creek, my boy. We do our killing for ourselves. Gun play ain't no more popular here than a rattler in a tea party. Why, one good killing up here and we'd have more law than we could choke a bull. Our whole party would be plumb spoiled. You go along and step soft and be a good boy."

So, with a playful little shove, he started Lee Garrison on his way into Crooked Creek.

13

HE had been too closely intent on changing his appearance to pay much heed to the town up to this point, but now he stepped out to observe and be observed. There was momently more to see, for now, as the evening drew closer, the men were beginning to come in from the mines. They were very much alike in spirit. Whether they had seen much or little yellow metal in the work of the day, each carried a high head and looked about him with a possessive eye; for having been lately familiarized with magic visions of gold, all desirable things were only around the corner in their hopes. There was plenty to engage the mind along that twisting, angling street of shacks and tents. The moment the news of the gold strike was verified, three jewelers had rushed extensive stocks to the valley; now they were arrayed side by side, each vying with the other in the magnitude of his display in the unglassed windows. To guard the wares, two hard-faced men with sawed-off shotguns stood near. They had enough lead under trigger to wash the solid crowd from the street.

These windows drew a continual audience in which the men stood in deep quiet, nearing the sparkler of his choice. In fact, the jewelers obtained a fat revenue from those who felt that the door of opportunity would open for them by the next day, at the latest, and made deposits to hold for twenty-four hours the dazzling transparency of a diamond.

Lee Garrison peered for a while between heads and shoulders at the display, then turned with the rest to watch a monster wagon lumber past, drawn by twelve mules, which leaned wearily into their collars. It was like a big ship in a small harbor. It fairly filled the street and jammed the crowd back on either side. The top of the load was well above the level of most of the roofs, and a shouting boy of twelve stood on the very crest, swaying back and forth against the sunset colors as the wheels, far below, dipped into the ruts through pools of dust. Besides the driver, who rode a wheel mule and managed the long jerk line in his left hand with the air of a master, there were six men who walked in a company before the team, waving their hats and yelling to the bystanders. A victorious troop of cavalry could not have raised a noisier jubilee or more dust.

"That's what I call a pretty turnout," said a man beside Lee. "That's coming to dig in style, I say!"

"But style's not the only thing that counts," suggested Lee.

"Some liquor on that," said the miner, turning the weather-hardened face of one who has lived his fifty years in the open. "Couldn't be truer if you took it out of the Bible."

He hooked his arm through the arm of Lee.

"Look at me," he continued as they went on. "I come with the price of a pick and a prayer. Hit the stuff the second day; been in bonzana ever since." His head jerked back with exultation. "After all these years!" said the miner. "After all these years!"

The crowd immediately before them slowed and thickened around the only glassed windows in Crooked Creek, the windows which framed the brilliant display of the leading

94

haberdasher of the moment. Gold and bronze and green and
red and burning orange, the neckties and scarfs and silk
shirts flamed like autumn foliage of fiery mid-October.
Against that glowing background stood a full-length model
of a gentleman in evening dress, most formal from glimmering top hat down the broadlike front of the shirt, relieved
with ruby studs, to a waistcoat made snug above an
incredibly slender pair of hips, and so on to the trousers,
pressed to knife-edge creases, and patent-leather shoes. The
dummy clasped white gloves in one pink hand, and the
other—most lifelike—was raised to toy with the stately,
wide-sweeping mustaches. Lee's companion puffed out his
chest and drew in his chin, an unconscious imitation.

The crowd kept silent.

"There's a high stepper, eh?" murmured the miner.
"Now, how d'you think I'd look, turned out like that?"

"Fine as silk," answered the sympathetic Lee. "But do
they ease around in togs like that in Crooked Creek?"

"Not yet. That's here for an ad, I guess. But one of these
days they might start dressing up in the Frog Dump."

"What's the Frog Dump?"

"Monsoor Lefevre's dance hall. He's got a slick place.
Here's another holdup!"

They heard a droning voice, so cunningly pitched that it
floated through all the uproar of the crowd, and immediately
they passed a white-headed man who bore in a tall legend
upon his hat the following: "Blind by a powder burn. Please
help." The beggar extended alternate hands, for no sooner
was one stretched out than it was filled with broad pieces of
silver or rustling bills. Lee's companion pressed a large
donation into the clawlike fingers.

"First real, honest-Injun blind man in Crooked Creek,"
he said with pride as they went on. "Trouble is he's making

so much money he can afford to retire pretty soon, and then we'll lose him. Hel-lo."

A crackling stream of curses, loosed by a shrill voice just in front of them, stopped the drift of the crowd, jammed it back, and then split it into a score of confused groups as though with an explosion. Lee Garrison saw a little red-headed man with his hat hanging on the back of a very long, narrow head. That head jutted forward as though its weight were too great for the supporting neck. Drunken rage rocked him back and forth, and he reminded Lee with horrible vividness of a mad dog he had once seen with frothing muzzle and bloodshot eyes. His curses were driven at the head of a youth who was obviously certain that he was about to die, and who was obviously determined to die rather than run.

"It's Red Billy Devine," said Lee's companion. "You and me'd better be sidetracking it, son. They'll have their guns out pronto!"

But now another man began shouting from the far side of the street: "Hey! Hey! Cut that out!"

Behold the fat barber waddling through the crowd like a sheep dog through a flock! All the body of Red Billy was shaking with passion, save his right hand only, and that was locked around the butt of his pistol until the instant that his stream of insults should induce the boy to pull his own weapon. Let into the path of that impending lightning flash, the barber made his way straight to terrible Red Billy and laid his pudgy hand on the collar of the man of war. Amazement set the crowd gaping.

"Now look here, Billy, you little fool," said Gus, "what you mean by making all this noise? I sliced the gent I was shaving twice, listening to you holler!"

The wild eyes fastened on the face of Gus. "All I do is ask him for a measly hundred bucks," said the gunfighter. "He

96

says he ain't got it. Ain't got a hundred dollars! Why, ain't everybody here got thousands? Him with a white skin and talking white, but he wouldn't give me a hundred dollars!" His voice broke with sorrow. "Gus, how come a man can be as low as that?"

"You come along with me," commanded Gus. "You're drunk, that's what's the matter."

"Me drunk?" shrilled Red Devine. "Lemme show you how steady my hand is, Gus. Just lemme kill him—just that one skunk, Gus!"

"Not a one," said Gus. "You'd get a sheriff and a flock of deputies up here investigating, would you? They'd have this little old town starched as stiff as a Sunday collar."

"But he ain't a man. He's a hound, Gus. It cuts me all up to have something like him walking around making folks think he's a man."

"You shut up and come along with me," broke in Gus, and under the impulse of that arm, Red Billy turned and went with reeling steps beside the barber. The crowd flowed in behind them.

"That's nerve," commented Lee's new friend. "If I'd of had a gun I might of—but Gus, he has the nerve."

"Funny that Devine let him manhandle him, though," suggested Lee.

"Funny? Devine knew darn well he'd get shot full of holes if he tried to pull his gun. Gus Tree is fast as a wink. Here we are!"

While Lee digested the astonishing news of the fat barber's prowess, he was guided through a wide pair of swinging doors into a saloon and pressed among the drinkers, five deep at the bar. They reached a place where he could look into the only mirror which had as yet been brought to the camp.

"You get better liquor over to Monsoor Lefevre's," said

Lee's companion, who now introduced himself as John Patterson. "But they charge such prices that the darned stuff chokes me going down. Might as well turn some gold dust into your throat!"

Lee heard him in dim distance through a fog of his own thoughts, for the face which confronted him in the mirror and which sat on his own shoulders, was the face of a stranger. Smooth-cheeked, boyish, sullen of mouth had been the fence rider of that range far south, but now a lean, grim, straight-eyed man stood before him in the mirror. It was like falling asleep and waking with mind and soul wrapped in a new body. Somewhere in the quest for Moonshine, one self had died, and a new self gripped the whisky glass at the bar in Crooked Creek. The man in the mirror raised the glass, and Lee lowered it slowly.

"Fill 'em up!" he said to the bartender, and turned to look over Crawford's Place. It consisted of two sections. The first to be built had been the barroom itself, a sprawling shack of raw pine lumber which was now jammed with men. But the rear end of the original building had been knocked out and opened onto a long dance hall, with little tables and scores of stools along the sides, and a narrow dance floor down the center. It was not the hour for dancing, however, and here and there a random game of poker was in progress. The walls and roof of this second and larger portion of the establishment were canvas. Patterson pointed out Crawford himself, a burly ruffian who looked the part of an ex-pugilist, standing now between his dance hall and his bar, in a position from which he could overlook the entire crowd. He wore two guns and rested his hands upon the butts with what seemed to Lee an undue aggressiveness.

But, as Patterson explained readily, "He's got to show 'em that he's on the job every minute. They're only waiting to take an advantage. There's a dozen gunfighters in here this minute. Look yonder—there comes Bill Devine looking for more trouble. And there's Charlie Kirk, the murdering hound! And there is King Peters, himself. By heaven, I didn't know he was in town!"

He designated with awe a handsome youth who could hardly have turned his eighteenth year, but whose lordly manner and the elbowroom he was given at the bar proclaimed him a man of distinction.

"Why King Peters ain't hung, I dunno," muttered Patterson. "But with a gang of killers like that around, you can't blame Crawford for packing two guns and keeping 'em in sight. There he's sending old Bad-luck Billy Sidney to ask somebody to step out of the place till some of his liquor has evaporated. Good thing about Crawford. He don't let 'em get mad drunk in his place!"

Glancing again toward the proprietor of the saloon, Lee saw that he had just waved off on a mission an ancient fellow whose silver hair and shrunken body spoke of a full seventy years, at least. Yet he carried his tall frame as straight as any youth, the smile of a youth on his thin lips, and the fire of youth still in his little pale-blue eyes. Lee looked curiously after him until he was lost in the crowd which momently thickened. Every instant the swinging door flashed open and newcomers arrived from the mines. And one of the new arrivals was no other than little Buddy Slocum, now dressed in complete miner's costume of heavy boots and dirty slouch hat, with his shirt open at the throat. Every article was sizes too large and emphasized the more the weazened body of the ex-jockey. He caught sight of Lee at once, and his face contracted into a snarl of malevolence as he turned to mutter to his companion. The latter looked straight at Lee with the unmistakable glance of one examining a dangerous man.

There was no doubt that Buddy would noise Lee abroad as a crooked gambler.

To crowd that disagreeable thought out of his mind with another topic, he turned back to Patterson. "How does Bad-luck Billy get that name?" he asked.

"You ain't heard of him? Well, most everybody has. Been around for thirty years. Finds a man to tie to and starts making himself useful. Ain't got the gumption, somehow, to work by himself. And every man he comes to goes down and out sooner or later. That bad luck of his is catching. There was old Hugh Gummere. He dug so much gold he didn't know what to do with it all. But Billy Sidney came along, got him interested in irrigation, and he sunk the whole wad in three years. There was Hamilton Coster. He was the regular cattle king. He went broke about a year after Billy picked up with him. There's a long line of 'em. Never failed to be a Jonah wherever he went. But Crawford seems to be an exception. Billy found Crawford a bum, picked him up, got him on his feet, and now Crawford is making about a thousand a day out of this place and other things. He's made Crawford into a white man. There's a yarn that—"

His voice melted away in a hearty roar of applause which had risen from every throat in the room as the swinging doors were dashed apart and a huge man strode in carrying a boy perched on one shoulder.

"That drink sure rode well," said Lee to Patterson. "Sat right down in the saddle. Let's have another and tell me why they're busting their threats for that fellow."

But Patterson was gone from him and was working his way through the crowd to get closer to the giant.

In the meantime the latter had advanced to the bar and deposited the boy upon it, while dry-throated miners abandoned their drinks on either side to make ample room. Why such precious space should be turned over to the youngster was bewildering to Lee, for all he saw was simply an over-petted, over-pampered, over-dressed little invalid of six or eight years. He was turned out like a miniature cow-puncher, more gaudy than a rich Mexican. A sombrero of bright, blue velvet was belted with gold, worked into arabesques. A scarlet bandanna surrounded his throat, and beneath was a vest of soft fawn skin held together with big pearl buttons. About his meager hips sagged a cartridge belt mounted richly in gold, and the same metal appeared in the chasing on the butt of the tiny revolver which the belt supported, while the holster was red morocco, with a pattern worked on it in small emeralds! Below the gun, silk-corduroy riding trousers disappeared into red boots to match the holster. To top off an outfit which would have made the heart of an African king leap with envy, the tiny fellow carried a quirt whose handle was roughened with a profusion of jewels, that flashed as he pushed back his heavy hat with the whip.

But clothes could not longer make the child happy. His colorless, sullen mouth did not curve to a smile as he turned here and there and surveyed the smiling, cheering crowd with eyes at once fever-bright and weary. He was guarded against a fall from the bar by the great encircling arm of his companion. The latter measured from the floor well-nigh as high as the lad standing on the bar. He was as roughly dressed as any man in the room, with only one point of foppishness, this being the extreme nicety with which the black beard that covered most of his face below the eyes, was brought to a sharp point below the chin. For the rest, the upper part of his cheek shone like a red apple with the coursing of healthy blood. It seemed that the least fraction of his enormous overplus of health would have sufficed to cram the little body of the child with energy and high spirits. He took his hat from a head tousled with dense, black curls and waved it to the crowd.

"Charlie's struck it rich again, boys," he cried in a voice that made Lee start with many memories. "Charlie's landed in bonanza once more, and he's come to set 'em up for the crowd."

A growing bellow of applause nearly drowned the last of these words, and yet there was no reflection of the cheer in the sad little face of Charlie.

"Set 'em up, barkeep," continued the bearded man, "and hark to this, boys. Charlie tells me he knows they's some in camp that ain't had his luck, and he wants 'em to have another chance. He'll grubstake ten men today—the first ten that shake hands with him. Come on, boys. Who wants backing?"

The steady flow of high-priced liquor across the bar had seemed to indicate that every one was well enough found in money, but now a score of men came to vigorous life and squeezed, shouting, through the crowd to get at the out-stretched hand of Charlie. They closed with a rush around him, and, as their huge brown hands reached toward the boy, for the first time Lee saw him flush with pleasure. He danced back on the bar as far as the thick arm of his father would permit him, laughing and clapping his hands together, holding them high above his head so that no one could quite come to grips with him. The giant father looked up to the child, his face suffused with such joy that the black beard trembled; and, looking into his face from this angle, Lee Garrison remembered. It was Olie Guttorm, disguised only by the semi-foreign cast which the pointed trimming of his beard gave him. It was Olie Guttorm as he had been when he disappeared over the hill top with the chunk of rose quartz in his hand and his dark eyes ablaze on the trail of gold!

14

HE remembered still more. No wonder these mountains had seemed dreamily familiar, for the vision dream in which he saw them first was the nightmare of pain when he trudged among them on the trail of Moonshine. Had he not seen, at the head of Crooked Creek, the hill with the crown of white rocks? Yes, beyond question that was the place where he had picked up his sample. His directions had pointed the way to a fortune for Olie Guttorm, and Olie Guttorm's discovery had brought a gold rush into the hills. Lee felt very much as one who picks the small hole in the dam and in a moment sees it widened to a roar of water. No wonder that the crowd gave way, then, for Guttorm must be the patron saint of Crooked Creek, the fountainhead of all the riches of money and happiness that might pour from it.

A sigh escaped him. All this wealth, then, had been his for the choosing, and he had given it all for Moonshine. But the very thought conjured a mind-filling picture of the horse. And Lee was content. The first poison taint of envy slipped out of his mind, and he was even able to look around the barroom with an almost paternal satisfaction. He had more than money could buy. Money? All the money in the world would hardly be worth the joy of honest Olie Guttorm when he met his benefactor. There is no wine like self-satisfaction to warm the heart; Lee Garrison could not help thrusting his hands in his trousers pockets and teetering back on his heels.

In the meantime, shouting with laughter and eagerness, every down-at-the-heel gold seeker in the room crowded toward little Charlie Guttorm. One by one they dragged down his pipestem arms and enveloped his fists in great, brown hands.

"That's ten!" he shrilled presently. "There ain't no more! There ain't no more!"

And, shaking his head, he clasped his hands behind his back. Others were still herding in toward him, but Olie Guttorm, with a sweep of his thick arm and a bellow, stopped them short.

"Charlie says no," he declared, "and what he says goes. Being denied ain't good for him, is it, doc?"

The being so appealed to now sauntered forward from the outskirts of the crowd, slowly twirling a glass of whisky between thumb and forefinger. He seemed to Lee Garrison one of those men who pride themselves, above all else, on their coolness, unfailing in every situation. He had one of those round, small-nosed faces which never quite lose the boy look, and which persisted in Doctor William McLeod in spite of his fifty years and his gray hair, so thin that the red of his scalp showed through. He was jauntily dressed in knickerbockers and a tweed coat in which such blues and reds were woven that purple resulted, a cheerful and almost violent purple. The miners gave back before him, such was their respect and kindness for everything appertaining to Olie Guttorm, and even the unseasonable nature of the doctor's attire did not cause them to pass the wink and grin. Perhaps, decided Lee, they were accustomed to the doctor and his ways.

The latter had now paused, spreading his legs and tossing off half his glass before he spoke.

"Within limits, Mr. Guttorm," he said. "Everything in

measure. You continually ask me for an absolute yes, or an absolute no. My dear Mr. Guttorm, how often have I told you that in such a delicate case as that of little Charlie the absolute is precisely what must be most avoided. Discretion is what we must have, and the middle ground is that on which we must take our stand."

"What the devil, doc!" groaned Olie Guttorm, but in a tone rather of pleading than anger. "I sort of get your drift, but I always got to look through a blizzard of words to make out where you're heading. Right now—"

The doctor halted further speech by removing his left hand from his coat pocket and holding it up in protest. He then drank off the remainder of his potion and continued: "If you want brevity by all means! Charlie has had enough excitement. Take him home at once!"

Olie Guttorm swept Charlie off the bar and into the cherished strength of his arms.

"Right away quick, doc," he said. "I'm sure sorry!"

He seemed to be apologizing, but the doctor with a shrug of his shoulders turned his back on his patron and started for the bar. Meantime, little Charlie, writhed in the grasp of his father until one fist was free, and he shook this in the direction of the retreating doctor.

"You big hog!" screamed Charlie. "I hate you! 'N I'll get even—you wait! I'll get even with you, and—"

Here his rage relaxed sufficiently to permit him to pass into a wail of grief. He turned on his father and beat his fists, small and bony as the claws of a bird, into the face of Olie. The big man merely blinked under the rain of blows and then rendered Charlie helpless by pressing him gently into the hollow of his shoulder.

"It ain't nobody's fault but mine," declared Olie sadly to the near-by men who were protesting that they hoped

Charlie would feel no ill effects. "I should of knowed better than to bring him down here. But he wanted to show off his new clothes, and—"

Charlie writhed halfway around. "It's everybody's fault!" he cried. "And—and I don't want you to give any one of 'em a single cent of money, dad, you hear me? If you give one of 'em a single cent—I—I'll cry all night long and make myself—"

"Hush up, Charlie. Don't you worry none about nothing, son," said Olie. "I ain't going to do nothing that'll hurt your feelings, son. They ain't going to get a cent of money out of me!"

Charlie relaxed to a whine, while the father, reassuring the stake seekers with a wink, started again toward the door. Around him rose a chorus of thanks and kindly farewells that set the eyes of the simple fellow gleaming with happiness. It was while he looked around to collect this tribute of applause that his glance fell on Lee Garrison. All joy was wiped from his face. He hurried on with his head a trifle inclined.

Undoubtedly he had recognized Lee, but why that recognition should affect him so strangely the latter could not imagine, so he slipped into the path of Guttorm near the swinging doors and approached him with a smile.

"Olie Guttorm!" he said. "I guess you remember me?"

"Know you?" roared Guttorm so violently that his beard shook. "Sure I know you, and I don't know no good about you. Get out of the way and lemme pass!"

His thick arm brushed the other aside; the swinging door clicked behind him and fanned a warm breath of air into the face of Lee.

"Why, darn your thick hide, I'll teach you to re- member—" Half a dozen hands gripped him as he sprang in pursuit. They tore him back and jammed him against the wall.

"You'll teach him nothing!" growlingly answered one. "You wait till Guttorm has got his kid off of his hands, and then he'll handle you. But right now you'll leave him be."

The knowledge that he was so completely in the right and Guttorm so completely in the wrong, stifled Lee, as though he had been discovered in an act of most shameful imposture. They were honest men, these fellows, and as he confronted their hostile faces he knew that his story could never be believed no matter with how many oaths he swore to it. He would never dare to stand up before sane men and tell them that he gave up a gold mine for a pipeful of tobacco and liberty to pursue a mustang—on foot! An hysteria of rage made his wits spin. Olie Guttorm was far away and barred from him, moreover, by the devotion of every hardy man in the town; but within arm's reach were six or seven who had just laid hands on him.

The places where their fingers had gripped burned him, and by ill chance in that instant of quiet he heard a voice saying: "That's him that caught Moonshine. They been telling me that he's a gambler, too, and crooked as a snake!"

It was one of those murmuring voices which are meant for a single ear, only, but it was the spark which ignited all the gunpowder of Lee's fury. There was no volition in it. His fist of its own accord doubled, his arm lashed out, and he struck into the nearest face. He felt the knuckles bite through flesh to bone. His arm jarred from wrist to shoulder with a numb tingle, and under the shock the other went down. From around him a dozen men sprang, not at Lee, but to clear a space, for when a blow had been struck, guns must follow? But as for Lee there was no thought of another weapon than his bare hands, so much had rage blinded him, and when he saw the fallen man twitch a revolver from its holster his passion became pure madness. He ran straight in on the leveled Colt.

For an instant Fate waited.

The blind god of chance saved him from the bullet which hummed past his ear. He tore the gun from the prostrate man and jerked the half-dazed fellow to his feet.

"You yaller-bellied hound!" shrilled Lee. "Get out of this place and get out of the town. If I see you again I'll break your murdering neck for you. Start moving!"

Not until he had spoken did his brain clear, and his eyes. He saw that he was confronting no other man than that youth of wild fame, King Peters himself, and a prickle of fear worked up his spine. But King Peters was a man transformed. It is not a small thing, at the tender age of eighteen, to be looked upon askance by the law-abiding, to have one's lightest word or gesture noted, to discover a magic in one's glance which makes the eyes of strong men fall, to be robed with a repute which shakes the nerves of even the brave. And here was a stranger, an unknown, who had leaped on him like a tiger, knocked him to the ground, run in upon his leveled gun, escaped his shot by enchantment, torn the weapon from his fingers, and now threatened him with death if they met again. It was a glimpse into a new world for King Peters. That lordly courage which had been founded upon a knowledge of superior nimbleness of fingers and wrist, superior steadiness of eye, melted like a ghost at break of day. Fate, he felt, had overtaken him, and with a fallen head he shrank from the barroom.

There was a little murmur of taken breaths such as men draw when they have seen a shameful and a wonderful thing. To more than one that picture was like a prophecy, for how many of them had blustered a way among their fellows? And each rough-handed man saw a time coming when he should be mastered by some fiery and fearless spirit.

How could they tell that the most astonished man in Crawford's Place was Lee Garrison, and that it was the numbness of slowly departing fear which made him walk so slowly toward the door and slowly into the street?

15

"I SUPPOSE," said a voice behind Lee as he went down the street, dazed, "that you wish to be alone to get the relish of that situation in retrospect. But I hope you'll pardon me if I walk a step or two with you?"

It was the doctor, overhauling Lee with the long and rhythmic stride of a fine walker. He seemed flushed both by the exercise and with emotion as he drew up to Garrison. "I'm Doctor McLeod," he said in introduction. "You may not have noticed me in the saloon a moment ago, but you would hear of me if you stay long enough in Crooked Creek. They've been snapping at my heels ever since I began to take care of the Guttorm brat, which is time thrown away, medically speaking, but financially—well, one must live, you know. In the meantime, I can't tell you how it tickled me to the very midriff to see that fellow Peters handled. He browbeat me only yesterday in Lefevre's."

He laughed and whirled his cane with such dexterity that it flashed in the sun like a shining disk, and Lee noted the tapering slenderness of his fingers. But more than any physical attribute, it seemed to him that he had never seen a man who exuded such an aroma, as it were, of perfect rascality. He apparently had no care to conceal his nature from Lee.

"I should like to take your hand," ran on McLeod, "to thank you for that lesson to King Peters, but even the thick head of Olie Guttorm would turn suspicious if he heard that I had shaken hands with an enemy of his."

"And what will he think when he hears you took a stroll with me?"

"He will think what I tell him to think, as usual," said the doctor, "which is that I took this opportunity to advise you to leave town at your earliest opportunity because in going against the power of Olie Guttorm in this town you are going against a stone wall!"

"Look here—I ain't trying to bust Guttorm."

"No? Old friend of his, perhaps?"

"I'll tell you the straight of it, doctor. It was me that come across the outcropping of rose quartz up—"

He was interrupted by the suddenness with which the doctor turned upon him and by the bright-eyed gravity with which the professional man examined him.

"Really?" said McLeod. "You are the man who found the ore, and the cunning villain, Olie Guttorm, has beaten you out of your just half of the profits while you lay sick of a cold in the head!" Here he broke into pleasantly modulated laughter.

"By heavens, Garrison," he said, "I am not surprised to hear that you are such a wonder with cards. You have the face for the master poker player of the world. And if you possess the technique as well—tra-la-la!" He whistled a thrilling little strain of music and concluded by smiling benevolently upon Lee.

It was easy to understand why he opened his heart so quickly and so completely. He felt that they belonged to the brotherhood of knaves.

"That the hand that rocks the deck shall rule the world,"

paraphrased McLeod. "I sit in at a game occasionally myself, and I know a thing or two about the eloquence with which a pack may be taught to speak, but my great handicap is that I began too late in life. In cards as in music, those who hope to be masters must start early and continue long."

It would simply amuse the doctor to pretend to innocence. The story which the jockey had told of that game by the camp fire must have been eloquent indeed.

"Doctor," said Lee sullenly, "that little rat of a jockey has been telling lies about me, and you've believed him!"

McLeod chuckled with the utmost good humor. "My dear fellow," he said, "I have simply used my eyes. Someone was saying that you showed up in town looking as wild as a wolf. Well, my friend, the wolf look doesn't lie in long hair alone. You have had your hair cut, I see, but you have not taken the wolf out of your step. You walk like a man about to run a race; or like a man just out of prison and infernally eager not to get caught and sent back!" Here he probed Lee with a side glance, though he continued without interruption: "Though, of course, no prison could give a man a skin as brown as tanned leather and apparently as tough. But more than all this, you have a hungry eye, Garrison, as though you were questing for something—money—fame—woman—"

Lee started. He fumbled in his pocket the soft leather of the glove.

"Well?" McLeod was asking. "A pain from an old wound, or an idea."

"Both," answered Lee.

McLeod sighed. "You're a lucky dog with your youth and your flying start. You'll walk on smooth lawns the rest of your days."

Lee Garrison heard him out of a mist. He would lose that money he had won by playing cards the night before. He would go into "Monsoor" Lefevre's gaming house and throw away every cent of it. Then he would start out to work in the mines until he had laid up a handsome stake, and with it in his pocket—oh, comforting thought of money clean won—he would go again adventuring on the trail which had started from the ruins of the little hut under the cliff.

"Tush," murmured McLeod, "you are as secretive as a very mole, man, but—"

"Is that youngster, Charlie—is he Guttorm's boy?"

"He's Guttorm's boy. But there's none of Guttorm in him. He's all his mother's son, and like most of that ilk he's a whining, over-pampered little puppy. I have practiced facial expression most of my life, but, by heavens, I have nearly lost control of myself a dozen times. Every day I wonder if my tongue is about to stumble into ten words of the truth, and so kill the goose who lays the golden eggs."

McLeod spun his cane and whistled another refrain as though to drive the melancholy thought from his mind.

"Not really sick, then?" said Lee Garrison, relieved, for in spite of his anger he had pitied the man for the sick boy he loved so well.

"Sick?" repeated the doctor, and scuffed his heels jauntily. "Tut—he's dying!"

"The devil!"

"He is a devil in his own small way, and he'd grow up to wring the heart of poor Olie. He has another six weeks or so to linger along, or again, a bit of a shock, a cold, or almost anything might burn him out in thirty minutes." He made a gesture as though snuffing a candle.

"Poor Guttorm," sighed Lee. "It'll about break his heart, I suppose."

"Hearts don't break these days," said the doctor. "That sort of thing is out of fashion."

"Does Olie know there's no hope?"

"Of course not. That's why he employed me—the idiot! A dozen experts told him the truth. I heard about it, looked him up, and promised the boy long life and happiness—barring accidents."

Lee caught his breath.

"That surprises you, eh?" said the doctor, chuckling. "You know the tricks of your own trade—you'd clean out a parish priest of his last cent of charity money, but you cluck like a hen when you hear about my little game. Well, it's a neat one, at that."

"When you become a doctor," said Lee, "don't you have to swear to—"

"In heaven's name, lad," cried McLeod, "do you think I'm a real doctor? Practicing in Crooked Creek? Come, come, use your imagination. I'm no more a doctor than you, but I'm doing as good a job as the best doctor in the world, for I'm keeping the eyes of poor Guttorm closed to the truth, and that gives him happiness. Every day the youngster lives is a golden day for Olie Guttorm. Could the finest doctor under heaven improve on that? No, by the heavens, I'm his benefactor!"

He threw out his hands. "It's pure benevolence, Garrison! And now I'm afraid we must walk no longer together, for if I have simply been urging you to leave town because of the danger of Olie Guttorm, I could have crowded a very considerable expostulation into the space of our stroll, eh?"

McLeod laughed so softly that a person ten yards away would not have heard him. Withal it seemed a hearty laugh—of a sort.

"And you are going to stay, Garrison? You're not going to let public disapproval run you out of town?"

"I guess not," said Lee, waiting for the hidden thing in the mind of the pseudo doctor.

"Good," exclaimed the other. "As a matter of fact, while

we sauntered along, an idea has been growing in me. Of course I understand why you want to work Crooked Creek. There's oceans of gold here. Oceans of it!" His lips trembled over the words and his eyes shone. "They're drunk with wealth, Garrison," he went on. "And why should they have it? The yokels! They know nothing but labor and boozing, whereas—" Here he stopped short, glanced at Lee, and snapped his fingers.

"The point is this," he said. "When you are making your harvest, I happen to know that it is easier for two to work than one. You raise your eyebrows, eh? You are saying that it is only true when the two are tried friends and can trust one another. True again, Garrison, but if you decide to take a gambler's chance with me, it will pay you well—very well, on my honor! You are going to reap a great harvest—a great harvest! When I heard, in the saloon, about your skill with the cards, and then had a glimpse of your nerve in facing down the crowd—by Jove, I said to myself, Napoleon! But Napoleon needed marshals, Garrison. And you need a helper if you wish to make a quick reaping of the grain, and quick your work must be if you wish to escape from Crooked Creek before your past overtakes you in a tidal wave, or before some dozen of these gunfighters take the tidy thought of a murder into their hearts!"

How completely the clever man was making himself a fool, thought Lee Garrison, and on the spot he made a wise resolve.

"And now, Garrison, what d'you say? No reflection— quick, on the spur of the moment speak your mind for or against and never mind my feelings. Is it yes or no?"

Irritation, disgust with the false doctor, distress at his own strange situation in the mining camp, were all overwhelmed in a wave of mirth which began to rise in Lee. He managed to keep back the laughter, but he could not prevent the smile.

"Partner," he said, "you're sure welcome to sit with me at any little game I'm in."

"Ha!" cried McLeod softly, and his cane quivered in his grip. "That's good—that's darned good! The beauty of it is that they'll never suspect an underground wire between us two, not while I'm taking care of Guttorm's brat. But when do we get together and run over our signals? Or when can you let me know your system of daubing. I suppose you daub them, Garrison?"

Lee, who had not the slightest idea what daubing might be, coughed. "I'll be at Lefevre's tonight," he said. "You won't need signals if you play with me!"

The doctor parted his lips to speak, changed his mind, and coughed in turn.

"When you arrive at Lefevre's you'll find me in sight. Bon jour."

16

To have built in five minutes the reputation of a crooked gambler and a fighter was a bewildering thing to Lee. But when one has roused a nest of hornets it is wise to run, and he looked beyond the roofs of Crooked Creek to the mountains. Before night was thick he would be among them. He went straight for Moonshine. Rumor had already gone before him; a whisper spread on either side as he passed; he felt men behind him pausing and turning. But at last he was away from them all and behind Mrs. Samuels' house he had sight of Moonshine waiting for him in the rose of the sunset light. What a glad reunion it was from the instant the stallion caught sight of him and began plunging around the corral, until he came to a stop before his companion and knocked off the unfamiliar sombrero.

Lee Garrison, in an outburst of melancholy joy threw his arms around the neck of the horse and bowed his head against the shining mane.

"Oh, Moonshine," he groaned, "I've been a terrible fool, I've been ten kinds of fool. But we're going to get out of here. We're going to slide up them hills yonder and drop over on the other side into some place where we can be alone. Ain't I a fool to have been hankering after the sight of men? I got on tolerable well with just books, once, and now I have you, besides. And I'll try again—"

Here his voice, which had been trailing away, sank to nothingness, but behind his blank eyes his thoughts were speeding on to the conclusion that "Malory" and all the other books in the world would be a hollow comfort. The joy he had found in them was a ghostly thing, remembered, and all his past life was a host of shadowy days.

A whistle ran into his thoughts like the first thread of morning light into a room. He looked about, saw nothing, and wondered why his heart had leaped when he first surmised that the call might be for him. But who was there who could have cared to call him, after all? At the repetition of the whistle, therefore, he turned with greater indifference, and this time something moved in an upper window of the hotel, the only two-story structure in the town. The evening shadow had fallen so thick along that wall of the building that at first he made out only a misty form beyond the window, but that form now leaned into the light, and Lee Garrison was looking up into the face of a pretty, bright-haired girl.

"Hello," called the vision.

"Well," said Leé stupidly, "I'll be durned."

She settled herself on the window sill, leaning at what seemed to Lee a dangerous angle.

"You took off your hat to the horse," she continued, laughing, "and I think you might at least do as well by me."

The flash of the white teeth and the twinkling of her eyes had been pleasant, even in the distance. Automatically he dragged off his hat, so intent on her that he was heedless of his disordered hair, which the wind instantly blew erect on the top of his head.

"You've been watching me, then?"

"Don't flatter yourself, pal," said the lady, with an airy wave of her hand so that the lace of her dressing jacket fluttered behind the gesture. "A man hugging a horse is enough to draw a crowd even up here, where there ain't much but mountains to draw!"

And she laughed again, and suddenly he knew that the trail which started with the glove had ended with the face of this girl in the window. He wandered closer.

"You ain't going to leave if I stop looking, are you?" he asked.

Her laughter went out. She ended by shading her eyes and peering earnestly down at him.

"Where did you blow in from?" she asked. "What's your name?"

"Lee Garrison, ma'am."

She started to her feet at this. "You're him?"

"Have you heard of me?" he asked wretchedly.

She placed a hand over her mouth to shunt her voice in a new direction without turning her head from Lee. "Hey, Gertie. Come here quick, will you?"

Gertie's head presently appeared at the window; seeing

Lee she gasped and huddled her negligee higher about her shoulders.

"Hello," she said, to her companion rather than to Lee. "Found a friend?"

"I hope so," said Lee earnestly.

This threw the first lady into a gale of laughter. "He hopes so! Gertie, I want to present Mr. Lee Garrison!"

There was a squeal from Gertie. "Alice, you don't mean it."

She dropped both hands on the window sill and leaned far out, a dark beauty who, having entered the late thirties, used her make-up with more resolution than art, but in the dim light and the distance the effect was not altogether unpleasant.

"Tickled to meet you, Mr. Garrison," she called, fluttering her hand at him. "We've heard about your little party over at Crawford's. When are you going to look us up?"

"I'd like to drop around and call any time I may," said Lee.

They laughed again. They had the strangest habit, he thought, of laughing at everything.

"Come into Lefevre's tonight," said Alice. "I suppose you'll be making that headquarters, anyway! The Frenchy runs the only decent tables in town. When you're tired talking to the cards, come in and talk to us, will you?"

"Will I?" cried Lee, thrilling. "I'll tell a man I will? How soon are you going?"

"We'll be there when things start stirring, and they start stirring early in Crooked Creek. Lefevre's is going strong by seven thirty. We'll be there by eight. What time d'you expect to break up your own game?"

"My game?" Then he comprehended. They had heard of Buddy Slocum's tale. He was glad of the deepening shadows. "I'll see you at eight," he managed to say, and waved to them as he turned away.

They shouted farewell in musical chorus, and then he was around the corner and mercifully alone. A crooked gambler! He dug his finger nails into his palms in the bite and sting of his shame. But they had liked him, it seemed, in spite of his profession—how thick they had showered their kindness upon him!

He would prove himself worthy of their esteem, he vowed. Before he met them he would throw away his money at Lefevre's tables, and then meet them at eight o'clock with clean hands!

Behind him, as he left, Moonshine neighed frantic protest at this new desertion, but Lee Garrison hardly heard the sound. His mind was crowded with memories of music of quite another nature. But when he was close to her, what could he find to say to so lovely and brilliant a creature? He drank deep of the chill cup of humility; truly fortune had been blindly kind to him! He had found her in the very moment when he was about to desert the trail. He killed what time he could eating supper in the restaurant, and as he stepped from the door a man touched his arm.

"Guttorm wants to see you," he whispered behind his hand. "He's out in his hoss shed behind his house—the red house at the end of the street, if you don't know."

He disappeared around the corner while Lee turned in the bidden direction down the street, passing through the yellow bars of lamplight which struck out from the open doors. Overhead the darkness pressed flat against the roofs of the town, for the sky was massed with clouds, and not a star showed through. Yet Lee was singing softly when he came opposite the big, sprawling house of Guttorm. He paused by an open window on his way toward the horse shed, and inside he saw little Charlie and McLeod. Charlie was wrapped to the chin in a brilliant Indian blanket in whose folds there seemed more strength than in the small body they surrounded. His head lay back against a pillow, and in his pinched features there was a dying wanness. The "doctor" walked to and fro with his hands dropped in the pockets of his coat, talking steadily, though Lee could not make out what he said.

The eyes of Charlie opened, savagely discontent. "Stop!" he commanded. "I don't like it. I hate that story!"

"Shall I leave you, Charlie? Do you want to stay here and rest by yourself?"

"I want another story, with bears in it!"

"A man hunting bears, eh?"

The dull eyes of Charlie gleamed. "Or how bears hunt a man," he suggested.

The last was hardly above a whisper, but Lee understood, because he was half expecting exactly those words. He started on just as the smooth, pleasant voice of the doctor began again.

On one side of the horse shed there was a light, and going toward it Lee found Olie Guttrom seated cross-legged on the ground, busily at work with awl and waxed thread, repairing harness. As he sewed, he whistled softly. Now, for a moment, the burden of wealth had slipped from his shoulders. It touched Lee far more than the sight of the dying boy. He was strangely unable to be angry with the big man.

At his approach Olie Guttorm rose solemnly to his full height, and the lantern cast his sprawling shadow over the wall beside him. He scowled upon his visitor.

"Look here, Olie," said Lee, "you think that I've come to Crooked Creek to make you trouble. You're wrong."

He paused placatingly.

"Good!" said the miner. "That's good!" He rubbed his hands. "You want a share of what I've made out of the mines, eh? Well, it's coming to you. I might say that I bought that ore and that location from you fair and square with the tobacco; or I might say being as how I was drifting along in that direction, I'd have found that ledge myself in a few more hours. But I never dodge a debt. I pay up. Nobody could buy Crooked Creek with a pinch of tobacco." He had advanced to Lee, and now he dropped a hand on the latter's shoulder.

"Still wrong, Olie," said the younger man. "Darned if you ain't all wrong. I don't want money that I ain't worked for!"

Olie Guttorm stepped back, lifting his hand from Lee's shoulder and hanging it in the air as a great fist, hard and jagged as a rock. Slowly the fist dropped to his side.

"I thought it'd be this way," he said growlingly. "You want to get the credit for the Crooked Creek strike!" His whiskers bristled. A black vein swelled on his forehead.

"You don't understand," Lee insisted. "I don't want—"

"You lie!" gasped out the giant, glancing furtively around him. "Don't I see what's inside your head? You want 'em to cheer you the way they cheer me. You want to make me out a liar. But you're a fool to hold out for that, because I'll give you more money than you ever dreamed of, if you'll get out of Crooked Creek and never come back."

"I been telling you that I won't take money, and—"

"Wait, wait!" pleaded Guttorm. "You dunno what you're about to say. I ain't talking about a few hundreds. I'm talking about hundreds of thousands to you, Garrison! Will you listen to me, partner? What does it mean to you? You're young, and if you got money a-plenty you can make a name for yourself later on. But think what it'd mean to me if the truth got out about how the strike was made! Why, they'd despise me! All them that have been talking as if I'd given them what they've dug up. Garrison, if you go inside the house with me I'll show you sacks—"

"I'll come back and talk to you tomorrow," said Lee, backing toward the door. "You don't get my drift at all, tonight. All I been trying to say is that you're welcome to—"

He was unheard. "Then go and be darned to you," cried Guttorm. "I've made a good offer. I'd give you a quarter, a third, of it all. But you want—get out!"

With the last words his voice swelled to a roar, and he rushed at Lee with his clenched hands raised. And Lee Garrison fled without shame as one would flee from a beast. He raced through the darkness to the street, found himself unpursued, and slackened to a walk, panting.

They were all mad, it seemed. The whole town was filled with the insane. If only the girl were not here, he would throw his gambler winnings into the dirt and not wait to get rid of them at Lefevre's. But now that meant a diverting way of killing time until eight, that hour for which the world was waiting.

17

A SEARCHER for noisy excitement in Crooked Creek after dark would have passed up Lefevre's amusement palace for Crawford's, or one of the score of other saloons. And in fact, fully as many jammed their way into Crawford's as passed through the wide door of Lefevre's. For the Frenchman had established a law of silence in his gaming room, and though the quiet kept out many a merrymaker with a pouch full of gold, Lefevre had found that in a hushed room the bets run higher and men feel that fortune is leaning behind their chairs.

The result was that there were few quarrels over the tables in Lefevre's place, though a good many happened within twenty yards of his door. As midnight drew near, to be sure, there was a pronounced increase and sharpening of voices in the dancing section, but the moment that Lefevre's big clock struck the first chime for twelve o'clock, every game stopped, every dance ended, and the guests must start elsewhere.

If, at that hour, they went into Crawford's across the way, the contrast was sure to react most favorably in his behalf. But, at any rate, he was building up a repute which would make him strong as a rock when, as must inevitably happen, the town grew more settled and law and order became an invited guest. Then the past of Crawford's would rise in a black wave and sweep it away.

When Lee turned in from the street through the little grove of whispering aspens which Lefevre had so wisely left standing, and which gave so much privacy to his house, a voice called softly, and "Doctor" McLeod appeared from among the trees.

"I'm ready for the raid," said McLeod.

"How much have you brought along?" asked Lee.

"Five thousand," said the other.

"H-m-m," murmured Lee. "Did you get all of it out of Guttorm?"

"That and more. Everything that touches him is gilded. He is all gold! But by the way, that was rather a raw rub you gave the idiot."

"What?"

"He came raving into the house a while back and told me

that you have threatened to claim the honor of a prior discovery of the Crooked Creek ore, and that you are going about the town swearing that you met him when you were famished and sold your knowledge to him for a pipeful of tobacco. He's nearly mad; he ramped and raved through the house until Charlie began to squeal—confound him! And the last I saw of them, Guttorm had the brat on his knees and was rumbling a song that sounded like a cart rolling over a bridge. But whatever your game is with Guttorm, you're pressing him pretty far. The big chap will be running berserker one of these days."

"I have a grudge against him," said Lee, "and I worked up that yarn to worry him."

"It sounds almost queer enough to be true. You have an imagination, Garrison, by heaven you have! And now for tonight. What's the plan? How can you use me? I suppose you'll play poker?"

"No, the machines."

"Good heavens, man, can you use me playing the machines?"

"You're welcome to what you win," said Lee, smiling. "Follow me and bet where I bet."

"But the machines—" began McLeod in anxiety. "You have a system?"

"Sure."

"No doubt, but every system I've ever heard of—"

Lee Garrison cut him short by stepping through the door and into the hushed interior. He saw at once that the silence at Lefevre's was maintained as a game by the miners. They stalked about with gliding steps, and where one of their fellows landed with a heavy heel or exclaimed in an unguarded moment, a score of heads were sure to turn toward him. The floor itself in the gaming section of the house was of a nature to induce silence, for it consisted of the heaviest canvas stretched over the unsmoothed timbers beneath. Canvas, again, formed the roof, for a timber roof would have been far too ponderous to be supported by the meager uprights, which, for the most part, were simply straight saplings with the limber lopped off.

As for the arrangement of Lefevre's, it was both simple and effective. One half of the place was the game room, scattered full of card tables at the sides, with the gambling machines in the center. At the rear of the room was a long bar well equipped with white-clad bartenders against the background of a thousand bottles of a thousand dyes. The bar extended out of the game room and into the other half of the building, that is to say, the dance hall. Through the big swinging doors Lee glimpsed a polished floor, waxed, and rubbed until it picked up the reflections of the lanterns and carried them to dim and watery depths. Moreover, the lights in the dance hall were so much brighter that the shaft through the door struck into the game room as into semi-darkness. He saw a swirl of color moving across the floor, with shadows in pastel shades underfoot. And in the dance music there was no bray of brass such as tore the ear at Crawford's across the street, but singing violins ruled the orchestra.

Dulled by the intervening wall, the one solid and abiding feature of Lefevre's house, the music came dimly into the game room, a moan of strings, a faint whistle of the clarinets, or the pulse of the drums, so that varying melody pervaded the air of the game room.

On four things Lefevre spent with a prodigal hand—his music, his waxed dance floor, his liquor, and his gambling equipment of tables and machines. In his house men dallied with chance, lured and prompted to carelessness by the promise of the distant music. If they lost they sought courage at the bar and returned to the gambling table to lose with greater rapidity. If they won, they went to the bar to celebrate the victory and returned to the table with a dazed brain and lost. But in the end they arrived at one of two stations; either they had spent all but the fag end of their stake and sought the dance hall to go broke in style, or else, as winners they went for a few turns in the hall to display their wealth. But no matter what they did or where they turned, the net of Monsieur Lefevre was spread, and small were the winnings which escaped through the doors of his establishment.

To Lee Garrison the music was like a breath of perfume. It was a promise of Alice, and if she had been lovely as framed in the darkness of the window, how thrice more beautiful in the splendor of that shining room beyond the door!

In the meantime, as Lee drank in the scene, smiling with half-drunken joy, McLeod had drifted to a little distance, letting himself be carried along by the next eddy that came through the door. It was the expectancy in his glance which aroused Lee Garrison to the memory that he had come for a distinct purpose. No doubt to McLeod the smile of Lee was that of one looking down on the battlefield where he sees victory.

That thought made Lee laugh aloud. And this was to be the second time in his life that he had gambled! What should he try? Where should he lose his little fortune? There was one main center of interest among the machines. The chuck-a-luck table languished with only two or three dogged patrons. Faro had its meager half-dozen advocates. But the thick group in the exact middle of the room surrounded the roulette wheel. Lee Garrison made for it. From the side came McLeod, his face dark with doubt.

Lee swallowed a smile. He would begin in a small way; but he hardly knew how to play the machine. There were colors on each side of him marked off in little squares in which bets were laid. There were also squares on which numbers were marked. On one of these a neighbor deposited a dollar; and Lee promptly put ten dollars on the adjoining spot, covering the figure nine. From the corner of his eye he saw McLeod hesitate, and then shake his head. Evidently this was water too deep for him. Now the wheel spun, slowed, and stopped with a click. His neighbor's dollar disappeared under the expert stick of the man behind the wheel; but upon his own ten dollars, an instant later, three one-hundred-dollar bills and six tens were deposited. He had been paid thirty-six for one!

A flurry of placing bets recommenced. The man behind the wheel in a quiet voice was urging his patrons to get their money down more quickly, but Lee chiefly heard the man beside him saying, "Heaven a'mighty, stranger, you letting her ride?"

"Not this time," said Lee, and shifted his pile to the spot. The wheel spun again, hissed, slow, and stopped with a gentle click as the ball dropped. But this time the stopping of the wheel brought a great commotion. A dozen people were talking at once. Something had gone wrong, perhaps? There was a protest?

The immediate companions of Lee had pushed a few feet back from him, and all eyes were fastened steadily on him for a blazing moment of envy and surprise. The man behind the wheel, in the meantime, after deftly taking in the lost bets, began as swiftly paying the winners. Three or four had won on the color, two on the odd, and now he placed a neat pile of double eagles before McLeod, who was utterly colorless except for a purple patch high up on his cheek. After that the payer flashed over his stacks of money swiftly;

then sent an assistant scurrying across the floor. He seemed to spread silence with him; the news ran along invisible wires of rumor; the card games came to a pause, and the heads of the players turned. And again it was Lee who was the focus of interest.

"I've seen it tried," said Lee's nearest companion, "but this is the first time I ever seen it worked. Two times running. And here comes the old man!"

The messenger, walking heavily under a burden, was returning at the rear of a portly man who padded across the floor on little short legs and ridiculously small feet. He nodded to patrons on either side with a courtly gesture to accompany each salutation.

"Ain't he the game old sport?" said the murmurers around Lee. "Old French himself is coming out to pay. Maybe he wants you to take his note, Garrison!" But here was Lefevre, extending his hand. Lee's fingers sank into soft, cold flesh.

"I've heard of you before, Mr. Garrison," said the proprietor, "and I've been hoping that we should see you here. I see that you have made your own welcome, in a way—" Here he laughed a little and was accompanied by the polite murmur of the crowd. "But though I am a little late, let me add my congratulations, sir!"

So saying, he took a heavy canvas sack from his messenger and gave it to Lee. "Thirteen thousand, three hundred and twenty dollars," he said, loudly enough to be heard distinctly for some distance, "and now won't you drink with me?"

Lee found himself carried off in the midst of a hearty muttering of applause for Lefevre. Lee Garrison protested. "I sure hate to do this, Mr. Lefevre," he said. "The luck—"

"Tut, tut," the gambler assured him with a handsome frankness. "It is the fortune of war. Today you win and tomorrow I win. Do not pity me, Mr. Garrison, but be happy without a cloud. There are some poor fellows who creep out of here with their heads down and their last penny gone. On my honor I am sorry for them, and they know they can come to Lefevre for help, but their honest Western pride forbids that, it seems. However, Mr. Garrison, you will go out in a different manner. To your good health, sir, though I'm afraid I can't drink to your continued luck!"

The remark set the crowd laughing as their glasses flashed to their lips—a roomful of men, and a streak of crystal light rising in every hand, for when Lefevre treated, the whole house drank.

He would not accept a drink which Lee offered to buy, however, and immediately left the room. If some one had proposed a cheer for the proprietor at that moment, it would have been given with a mighty will. So gracious did he seem that it threw a peculiar imputation of craft and unfair cunning on Garrison by contrast, a slight cloud from which Lee could partially extricate himself by leaving the odd three hundred and twenty dollars with the bartender "to treat the boys when they looked downhearted!" Even this royal generosity made only a slight impression, for a big winner in gambling is too envied to be liked.

If he had instantly and joyously devoted himself to the labor of getting drunk in celebration, he would have been looked upon with a more kindly eye, but the complete daze in which Lee found himself was misinterpreted as professional nonchalance. If there were needed proof of Slocum's report that Garrison was a seasoned expert, it was herein provided. But Lee was not thinking of the opinions of others. That unworldly mind of his was merely grasping at the fact that he had come here to rid himself of money which was too unclean to be carried into the presence of the girl.

He sighed and looked around into the smoke-blue atmosphere of Lefevre's; every light was encircled by a luminous, milk-white fog. Yonder was McLeod, idling in front of a crap table, but he was keeping strict watch on his master. Lee Garrison made straight for that table, counted out fifty twenty-dollar gold pieces, and wagered them against the point of the house, which was eight. That thousand vanished. He replaced it, and the next thousand was swept away. He repeated for the third time. At one side he saw McLeod, who had been following these bets in a smaller way, break into a perspiration that made his face gleam, and Lee, as his fourth thousand disappeared, laughed joyously and bet again. He heard a murmur which said: "So sure of his system that he don't give a darn! That ain't gambling—it's gold digging. I told you so!"

For as he spoke, Lee won, let his bet ride, and won again, doubled, recouping his losses at a stroke.

And then he settled down seriously to the work of throwing his money away.

18

BUT the curse of Midas had descended upon Lee Garrison unasked, and whatever he touched turned into gold. At faro, to be sure, he managed to lose five thousand in a moment, but when he won on the next turn of the card he turned away in despair, while the man at the deck gaped to see the gambler leave at the very moment his luck changed. From faro he went to chuck-a-luck, where, having placed his accustomed thousand on the five, instantly two fives danced to the top in the next cast, and when he left his stake and winnings in the hope of seeing them disappear—they doubled again!

After this he went from table to table, literally throwing money away, but though he lost here, he won there. He could not even carry his winnings about with him, for gold coin weighs ninety pounds to every ten thousand dollars. So he hired one of Lefevre's own men to stand guard over that precious canvas bag while Lee went about with sack pockets sagging with a load of gold. But though he sowed it by blind handfuls, he could not lose it. At eight o'clock he had to shake his head in surrender. Alice, without stain and without reproach, was waiting for him, and he must go. Gloomily he started for the dance hall, with twenty times the money which he had come to lose. He passed the ecstatic form of McLeod, who had been exactly imitating the betting of Lee on a smaller scale, and who now muttered, "You're a master, Garrison. Nobody under heaven could make out your system; I've racked my brains over it and got nothing but—cash!"

That was the common sentiment. They had seen greater winnings in Monsieur Lefevre's, but they had never seen winnings taken in with so careless a hand. And what a system it was, which, in the space of fifteen or twenty minutes allowed the master to turn at will from one game to another, so completely the lord of all that it seemed his will was imposed on the whirl of the roulette wheel and on the arrangement of the faro pack! This, combined with his youth, and then the known facts about the affair at Crawford's, caused them to stare joylessly after him as he reached the big door leading to the dance hall, paused there a moment, and finally with a lift of his head disappeared into the brighter atmosphere of the adjoining room.

Lee saw her instantly, whirling in a yellow dress, or was it beaten gold made to flow soft as spider web about her? She spun down the center of the room in the arms of a handsome youth. The music, as though to greet his entrance, climbed in a rich crescendo, and the pulse of the drum grew hurried. She danced with a glistening arm outstretched, sheen in her hair, her face flushed. Then he looked more closely at her companion.

He was magnificent; he stood, one knew at once, exactly the romantic and perfect height of six feet. He was in the poetry of the early twenties, so that a woman could call him either man or boy, as her cunning fancy chose. Straight as an aspen he was and shouldered like an oak. His features were of statuesque perfection, with the straight nose and the long, strong sweep of the jaw line which Grecian sculptors loved to strike out with their chisels. Considering that this magnificent fellow was set off by graceful dancing, easy manners, and above all by precisely fitted "Sunday" clothes, Lee Garrison had reason to pause and watch that radiant pair weave through the crowd. How deft, how careless a guide was this big stranger; and how could human brain at one and the same time conceive the elaborate passages through which his feet were going in rhythm with the galloping music, and, at the same time maintain a steady and smiling flow of conversation!

The heart of Lee sank. His own harsh features were shown to him in a mirror; cheekbones too high, eyes staring and sunken, chin too lean.

In the meantime heads were turning toward him. Every one of them knew him, so it seemed, and each glance was accompanied by a subdued murmur. No doubt they were rehearsing the episode in Crawford's. He groaned as he hunted for a vacant table along the side of the room.

A voice detached itself from the conglomerate murmur,

and there she came with the handsome youth only vaguely in view behind her. He would have known her by her radiant body, Lee decided, had her face been masked in black!

She took possession of him in a swirl of words and gestures. "Here he is! This is Harry Chandler. I told him I was waiting for you to come, and he's been taking care of me. Wasn't that sweet of him? Do you have to go right now, Mr. Chandler?"

Lee watched Harry Chandler in wonder and sympathy, wonder that so magnificent a hero should be dismissed in his favor, and because he knew how embarrassed, awkward, and venomous he himself would have been had he stood in the boots of Mr. Chandler. To his considerable amazement young Chandler showed no dismay or confusion whatever. He acknowledged the introduction with a nod, and while he ran an indifferent eye over Lee, he produced a cigarette, lighted it, and tossed the match toward a near-by table.

"Sorry we're losing the last of that dance, Alice," he said. "But tomorrow night is another night. So long!"

And he drifted off leaving Lee with the feeling that, though he possessed the field, the laurel had been denied him.

"Want to finish this out?" asked bright-haired Alice.

He shook his head, saying that he did not dance. For certainly he would not invite invidious comparisons between his clumsiness and the skill of Chandler. That declaration cast something of a cloud over her, in the midst of which she guided him to her table, and he presently found himself opposite her cigarette and her smile.

The golden mist was vanished from her—how small a wind of truth had been needed to clear it away. Lee was seeing Alice-of-the-window for the first time. Her blue eyes were a little faded, and about the corners was a tracery of weary crow's-foot wrinkles. Her mouth was wider than strict necessity required, and the upper lip was a little crooked, verging toward a faint sneer where an irregularity of the teeth pushed it up a trifle. To be sure her complexion was as delicate as the rose flush of Aurora, but its perfection was now, alas, swiftly explained. For, leaning back in the chair, she produced a rouge box and powder, together with a mirror, and, holding this at arm's length and turning her head critically from side to side, ten seconds of accurate work replaced her damp and ragged flush with a dry and even one, restoring the pearl to forehead and chin.

She closed the little case with a sigh of satisfaction and snuggled the chain over her hand again.

"A gentleman friend in Omaha gave it to me," said Alice. "He got tired of seeing me lose my bag, and so he went to a jeweler and got this thing. Ain't it sweet?"

"Sure," said Lee, leaning back as she leaned forward. "It looks pretty good."

A change passed over her as suddenly as the flick of a cloud shadow across the window. For a moment she studied him with coldly intent eyes, balancing a judgment.

Lee felt that disaster lurked ahead, and he did his best to stave it off by making conversation. "This Chandler you were dancing with—that's Handsome Harry, isn't it?"

"That's Handsome Harry," she answered. "He's a swell, all right."

And she looked past Lee with eyes made big by contemplating the full glory of Harry. And Lee himself was remembering stray bits of talk he had heard here and there about the town. This was the same man who had hunted Moonshine and, mounted on a wonderfully fleet mare known by the strange name of Laughter, had run the stallion for three days.

"He's got the blood," went on Alice-of-the-window, "and the blood tells. His father was a gentleman before him, and his grandfather before that. Old man Chandler came out here and started trying to raise thoroughbreds in the desert, but he went broke. Any real gentleman goes broke when he gets into business. All that poor Harry has is one horse and his face. But that one horse is Laughter. I guess you've heard about her. I've seen her!"

Alice's enthusiasm for Harry faded a little. She yawned in the face of Lee and leaned back in her chair. What might have happened then no one could have told, had not a man from the gambling room said to Lee in passing: "Celebrating, eh? They're still talking about how you cleaned up the games, in yonder!"

That sentence brought a delightful smile to the lips of Alice. She leaned toward Lee again with a dainty forefinger shaken in mock reproof. "So you've trimmed 'em, you naughty boy?"

He saw her rather than heard her. There had gathered over him a sick darkness of disappointment as he realized that Alice-of-the-window could not be the end of the trail which began with the glove and the shack. That gloom parted a little, and he saw her raised hand, and no more. Time, which had written of himself upon her face, had dealt gently with her hands. Her idle fingers, untrammeled by work, were girlish in slenderness, pink-tipped and pointed; and now he saw a palm of transparent delicacy, with a blue hint of veins. No matter if the golden vanity case which another man had given dangled from the round, small wrist. As though a wand had passed over him, Lee Garrison saw her again as she had been when she leaned above him from the window, laughing.

19

ENCHANTMENT, indeed, was there, and money was the enchanter. Not the lost trapper flagging on the trail when he sees the smoke twist above the unknown hills, nor the mariner when the light glints through the dark of the storm, is so transformed as was Alice-of-the-window by the thought of the gambler's winnings. There was no need of rouge now to stain her cheeks. Her eyes glistened, and her voice was sweeter. She was restored for a dazzling moment to what she had been when face and voice and smile mated that lovely hand. And Lee Garrison cast from his mind the first horrible suspicion. For that which was so beautiful must surely be good. Perhaps the glove in his pocket would perfectly fit that hand. Yet he was held back from the trial by a thread of doubt.

"Trimmed 'em?" he said. "Yes, I can't help winning. Money walks into my pockets even when I try to keep it out."

Her laughter was music, clear and sweet, "A good pick-up, dearie?"

Why did she use those foolish familiar words when she hardly knew him? However, he must not criticize. Words were nothing, and he would wash the strangeness from her talk.

"Whisky," he said to the waiter, "in a hurry." And to the girl: "Did I pick up much? Look!"

He thrust a hand into a coat pocket, and it came out dense and bristling with coins. Alice made a trembling, cherishing gesture.

"And lots more than that," said Lee. "Lots more. But it's bad stuff, Alice!"

"What sort of kidding d'you call that?" she asked a little hoarsely, and she strained her eyes away from that mass of money and forced herself to smile into his eyes.

"It ain't a joke," he assured her. "Money you get by gambling, money you get without work—well, it can't do you any good, you see?"

Again she laughed, just as she had at the window. Everything and anything made her laugh, and the sound flooded through him as the golden sunshine of a morning pours a room full of warmth.

"Ever hear of it doing any bad, Lee? You are a kidder!"

"But I mean—"

"Take a drink, dearie, and explain later; always do your drinking first. Here you are, Joe; and keep an eye on us, will you? My friend is dry!"

She picked up a twenty from the hand of Garrison and gave it to the waiter, who opened his eyes and fled before she should take back the donation. Lee swept the glass to his lips and then saw that she was drinking with him. Was that right? Should a woman drink? He forgot to wonder about that point as the hot stuff burned its way home in him.

"No chaser," he said, as she pushed the little glass of water toward him. "I like it straight; I like to watch the way it works inside."

"You're all man, ain't you?" smiled the girl. "I high-signed Joe to make yours double. I knew your style, honey!"

He harked back to the money. He must prove he was right. "What I said about getting something for nothing."

"Listen, Lee," broke in the soft voice of the girl. "I don't fall for that sort of stuff, honest. You don't have to pull the Sunday-school stuff to make me see that you're all O.K. If that money is poison—well, it'd sure take an awful mob of it to make me sick!"

"D'you want it?" he asked curiously. "Would you like to have it?"

Her eyes widened a trifle. "You can't tease me," she declared, and managed a rather shaky laugh. "I haven't asked you for it, have I?"

"If you want it, take it." He automatically caught up the refilled glass beside him and tossed off the dram. "Take it all! You know why I give it to you? You're too beautiful to be harmed by such stuff. Too beautiful and pure and good, Alice, for this dirty money to be bad for you. Gimme that bag."

She slipped it off with fingers that stumbled at their work, and she watched with incredulous, childish eyes as he opened it and then crammed into the interior a jumbled mass of money. It jammed the bag, swelling it stiffly, and still wide as it gaped, it could not swallow everything. Half a dozen coins dropped clanging on the table.

"If you want them," said Lee, "take 'em."

She began to gather the overflowed gold with a stilted pretense of a smile, ready to drop her spoil if he showed sign of anger. But there was no anger in him. He watched her with a smile as she packed the money tighter and tighter into the little golden vanity case and finally managed to squeeze the lips of it shut. She pressed it against her cheek and stared at him with a startled, happy look.

"You're wonderful," said Alice-of-the-window. "I never knew anybody as wonderful as you are, Lee!"

He shook his head energetically and drank again. The floor around him was alive with people who were moving out for a new dance, and they all traveled by ways which would bring them as close as possible to the table of Garrison, for

138

the whole crowd had seen the episode of the money. Their hearts might have been warmed at the sight of such foolish spending, but it merely angered them to see him throw away without thought what he had won, they believed, without risk.

And he was saying, "You don't understand, Alice. I ain't a gunfighter or a dead-sure gambler. Everybody's wrong. They don't really know me, you see. I'm as simple as any one could be. Never hunted trouble in my life and never learned a gambling trick or a gambling system. Will you believe me?"

"I'll believe anything," said Alice. "Why, you don't have to argue with me, Lee. If you want to kid me along, go ahead!"

She leaned back, smiling luxuriously, and lighted another cigarette. Immense hopes began to form in her mind. Who could tell? This man was something new. He was never serious, but he kept jesting with a strange, sober face. If she had not known a little about his exploit in Crawford's, she might have been duped, might have taken him seriously. She was worried by only one thing; why should he have chosen her above the rest? There were prettier girls in the room, younger girls. But she repeated to herself: "You can't judge a man by his choice of a woman. Besides, this cunning fellow is looking deeper than faces. He sees I ain't like the rest of these!"

Suppose, then, that his semiseriousness became true seriousness? Suppose that her fortunes were hitched to this wild, rising star? Two words rose in her mind, each with a thousand dream-bright pictures; Monte Carlo and Paris. She saw herself in a great hall, seated at a table covered with milk-white linen, liveried servants passing with muffled step or hung shadowlike behind the chairs.

Between two flickings of cigarette ash that dream poured through the brain of Alice; she had entirely forgotten the princely gift which now gorged her vanity case. There were greater goals ahead!

In the first place she changed her mind about one essential; she must not allow him to get too drunk. Granted that she could in this manner pluck all his winnings of the evening, she must not allow him to waken in the morning disillusioned, and so kill the goose of the golden eggs.

"I'm not kidding," he had said in answer to her last remark. She heard him distantly through her dream. "But we won't talk any more about me. I want to know about you, Alice. Tell me everything about yourself!"

He had opened a floodgate; it was her favorite topic.

It was later in that happy, happy evening, and her story was drawing toward its close. Thrice the saucer which held her cigarette ashes and butts had been changed. She had grown inured to the curious glances of the men and the wildly envious glances of the women. The table had become a throne to Alice, and her dominion was over the fire-eyed youth who listened so intently to her words. No doubt he was playing the game of cat and mouse, in a way, but to a certain extent it was impossible to doubt his sincerity unless he could continue to act a role and grow drunk at the same time.

For he was indubitably growing drunk! In spite of her cautioning, which made the tip-dizzy Joe cut the portions of Garrison to a mere wash of liquor in the bottom of the glass, the talk of Garrison became thicker. He articulated as though his upper lip had become numb.

"I ain't used to the stuff," he said, and she was forced against her will to believe him. After all, was it not true that most gamblers avoided drink?

"Time for us to be moving along, honey," she told him. "You're under the weather."

He protested stubbornly that he was sober as a judge. "But I'll go," he said, "as soon as you finish your story. You'd just got to the place where Crawford came up to you."

She fired with indignation as she recalled the incident, quite forgetting Lee, for the moment, except as a sympathetic listener.

"The big stiff walked up to me with that ugly grin of his. He says, 'You got to key down, blondy; you're making too much noise.' Can you imagine that? Him calling me blondy and telling me to key down? I was so mad I just give him a look until I caught my breath. 'Why, you big ham,' says I, 'if the floor of your dump was paved with faces like yours, it wouldn't be good enough for me to walk on!' "

Alice laughed a little as she recalled the brilliance of that retort. " 'Look here,' says Crawford, 'you do what I tell you—you key down or get out of my place!'

" 'Oh, is that so?' says I. 'I'll certainly be moving, then. The point is that you ain't used to having ladies in your holdup of a dive. But the day'll come, Larry Crawford,' I says to him, 'when you'll come begging me to pass a good word for you around among the boys,' says I, 'and then there won't be no noise about good talking!'

" 'Shut up,' says he, 'and get out! You're drunk!'

"I jabbed my heel into the foot of the flathead that was keeping me company that night. The boob was dead to the world. He'd been mixing his drinks. All I could do was to stand up and give Crawford one look and walk out."

Alice paused; the expression of Lee Garrison was part the daze of liquor and part bewilderment, with not nearly as much anger as she had expected. Had she said anything that might shock or offend him? She cast back over her remarks. No, her narrative had only been the spirited account of an indignity offered to a lady. Alice, herself, had been drinking a bit beyond her average.

She varied her tone. "And that's what I've come to, Lee. After my bringing up and the home that I was used to, that's what I've come to, a low-life like Crawford daring to— And what d'you think he said as I went out? 'Never come back!' says he. 'Your back going out is the most I want to see of you!' "

Lee Garrison dropped his fist on the table. "Did he say that? Why, the insulting hound!" Righteous indignation burned through him. The narration of Alice had been dim in his ears for some time, but now he recalled himself. She had been driven out of Crawford's by the proprietor—driven out by a man. Looking at her through a haze, the dazzling white of her arms and shoulders blinded him. Oh, cowardly brutality to have so shamed and maltreated this innocent and charming girl!

He started to his feet. "Meet me at the door," he said, and was gone.

20

APPALLED, Alice cried after him, but he was beyond reach, cleaving a downright road through the midst of the dancers and aiming at the door. Gertie swung out of a dance and appeared before her friend. She sent her escort on an errand to a far corner and so secured a moment for quiet chat with her companion.

"Well," she said, breathing hard from her exercise, "ain't

you got enough out of him? Can't you let him go now? I'd be ashamed, Alice, as greedy as that!"

Alice sank back into her chair. "Shut up, Gertie," she said. "You make me tired. Besides, you don't know nothing."

"Don't I? I know that you made a fat haul—unless he pushed some queer on you."

Alice gasped, jerked open the vanity case, hastily and critically examined some of the broad pieces with which it was loaded, and then sank back with a long sigh of relief.

"My heavens, Gertie," she said, "you might as well kill me as to scare me stiff! No, that boodle is straight stuff. The only thing that's queer is Garrison. I can't figure him—either a simp or a nut or a wise guy too deep for yours truly."

"A simp for blowing himself like that," said Gertie, her eyes dim with desire as she gazed at the vanity case. "But honest, dearie, how did you get it out of him? Or don't money mean nothing to that gold digger?"

"I dunno—nothing. My head's swimming."

"You better go home. I've got a lemon. I'll shed him and take you home; you been drinking too much, Alice." Gertie softened her voice to the gentlest sympathy; with Alice so suddenly flush it would be the height of folly not to establish the best diplomatic relations. But Alice shook her bright head decisively.

"He told me to meet him at the door."

"And you're going to? He'll be sober when he comes back, and he'll grab every cent he gave you."

Alice dropped her cigarette from lifeless fingers. But she recovered her assurance at once and shrugged her shoulders. "I'll stick," she declared. "You don't know him, Gertie. All I'm afraid of is that he's gone gunning for that fat pig, Crawford, and he may go after me if he comes back and finds me gone. Never can tell about a killer like him."

"My heavens, dearie," panted Gertie. "D'you mean to say he's gone to—and you ain't sent a warning to Crawford?"

"Warning? I would of stopped Garrison if I could, but now that he's gone, I hope he turns Crawford into a sieve. Why, what he said to me, Gertie—but I'm going out to see what's what."

She reached the door of Lefevre's barely in time to meet Lee Garrison with a gun belted around his waist, his hair blown awry by the night wind, his eyes flaring, his shirt opened to the air at the throat. And beside him was Moonshine! The left hand of the master twined in his mane steadied the frightened stallion. It was like hanging a sword from a thread, and Alice-of-the-window shrank away. A word had been passed. A crowd was flocking out of Lefevre's.

"You're coming with me," commanded Lee. "Get up on Moonshine, Alice."

"Oh, Lee—he'll tear me to bits if I come near him—he'll kill me, Lee!"

"Don't talk foolish, but gimme your foot. There you are. Moonshine, stand still!"

The stallion obeyed, but he crouched till he well-nigh touched the street in his terror. That made it easier to put the girl on his back, and there she sat sideways, clutching at the mane close to his withers to steady herself, and shaken violently by the tremor of the stallion.

"You keep quiet and you're all right," said Lee. "You ain't going to get hurt. Come along, Moonshine."

And the stallion, snorting and prancing, stole along beside the master. Lefevre himself, who had hurried toward the noise, had begun applauding, for he had a Frenchman's eye for effects. The example was followed with cheers and clapping of hands and stamping of feet, for, after all, it made a very pretty picture—the yellow-haired girl on that shining beauty of a horse, and the wild figure of Lee Garrison walking ahead.

They poured out behind the horse and into the street, while the broad shaft of light from the dance hall streamed clearly after them and showed the way to Crawford's place opposite. Straight on went Lee Garrison, reached the flight of half a dozen steps leading to Crawford's door, and behold Moonshine climbing those steps one by one, trembling with terror, but going steadily on in obedience to the hand on his mane. The applause became a roar. Men rushed for the doors and the windows of Crawford's to see the effect of that entrance.

The orchestra, chiefly brass, blared its music from the far end of the hall and kept a narrow maze of dancers in motion up and down its length, while packed tables on either side accommodated gamblers or drinkers.

Breaking through the rolling fog of tobacco smoke, the watchers saw man and horse and girl led straight down the hall, while the dancers packed back to clear a lane, and the music shrieked to a pause. Garrison stopped opposite the big chair in which Crawford sat enthroned, gross body, with his head inclined and his chin resting on his breast. In that position he continued for endless hours, rolling his glances from side to side and missing nothing.

At the sight of the horse and the woman he jerked up his head and shouted to half a dozen bouncers. But not a one moved. They were too intent on the words of Lee.

"I been hearing a pile of bad things about you, Crawford," said Lee. Before the sound of his voice a wave of silence spread, and even the watchers at the windows could hear.

"Mostly I've been told that you threw this lady out of your place, Crawford. Lemme tell you—in this part of the country you can't treat a lady like that, understand?"

From one end of the hall to the other rolled a deep growl of assent. It pleases the true Westerner to have chivalry attributed to him. He feels it to be just compensation for rough clothes, rough manners. Besides, there is a grain of truth in the fable, for there are fewer women than men on the frontiers. Now Lee was making himself spokesman for the honorable sentiment, and he received commendation accordingly. Crawford, rolling his bright little eyes up and down the double rows of faces, instantly saw the drift of feeling and determined to give way before it. He was a braver man save when courage interfered with business.

"Young feller," he said, "you're talking loud and long about nothing much. Who said that she couldn't come back here? Sure she can, and she's welcome!"

"Hear him crawl!" cried Alice. "He's yellow, too, the big four-flusher!"

"I sure misdoubt you, partner," said Lee with much gravity. "But I'm here to state that the lady's come back because she felt like coming, and she's going out again when she feels like going, but first there's an apology coming to her. Lemme hear it!"

The hand of Crawford twitched halfway to his gun—and paused. A remembered picture had crossed his mind of terrible young King Peters lying on the floor of his saloon that very day and shooting from the hip while this wild man, barehanded, ran in on him. The perspiring face of Crawford grew pale as tallow. In a great distance he saw the scorn in the faces of the men around him, but grimly near at hand were the fingers of Garrison, trembling just above the butt of his gun.

"Why," said Crawford, "I'm sure sorry if the lady's feelings have been hurt."

"That's enough," said Garrison, and he turned Moonshine back toward the door. He did not see Crawford roll out of his chair and tug out his gun. He did not see two of Crawford's own bouncers throw themselves on the man with curses and tear the weapon from his hand. It seemed to Lee that the uproar through which he passed was all a thunder of applause for Moonshine and the adorable beauty on his back.

It seemed to Alice, as they came out under the stars again, that it was the greatest night of her life. She could feel beauty, which had vanished ten years before, returning to her now, untarnished. And she began to feel both gratitude and awe for Lee. He was partly drunk and partly "different," but he had placed her in an epic light tonight. She had been only one among many in the evening. In the morning she would be famous.

As for Lee, the fumes of the whisky were mounting more and more to his head, and though the excitement of that incursion into Crawford's had nerved him, still alcohol colored all that he saw and did. And, as it operates on many nervous temperaments, it made him white of face and bright of eye as he started across the street for Lefevre's again with his way fenced in on either side by men and girls from both dance halls, by other townsfolk who had been attracted by the uproar, and, in fact, by every one who happened to be astir in the town. There were even half a dozen gaping children, drawn out by the uproar, and girls dressed brightly, and scores of laughing men. Immense brotherliness welled in him. They had misunderstood him for a time, but now there was more applause than criticism in their laughter—even the formidable old barber was chuckling and nodding approval. Indeed, among them all there was only one who sneered—Harry Chandler, who now drew back with the girl who stood beside him. But it was not the sneer of Handsome Harry that cleared the whisky from the head of Lee Garrison. It was the face of the girl beside the big fellow. For this was she whom he had hunted. She was the incarnate thought which had sprung into his mind when he had found the glove in the distant cabin, and the sight of her was to him like a friend's voice heard in a foreign land. Only a glimpse of her beauty and her scorn. Then she turned with Harry Chandler. But even with her head turned there was something sadly familiar. It was as though he had known her once and had been close and dear to her. And in her place sat Alice-of-the-window, on Moonshine.

He turned and looked up to her. Oh, fool, fool, fool, to have thought that this was the goal of the quest, or even a station by the way!

21

SICK at heart, he turned Moonshine up the street through the jam of people which split away before him. He was suddenly beyond the crowd.

"Lee, Lee!" called the anxious voice of the girl. "I can't wander around without a coat. I'll freeze. Go back to Lefevre's."

He looked around. The entrances of both houses of pleasure were black with returning people; already their uproar and exclamations were far off and blurring like something half remembered. He did not speak at once, and Alice, in quick alarm, slipped from the back of the stallion and came to him.

"What's wrong?" she asked anxiously. "Are you sick, Lee? Don't look back there at them—look here at me."

"Yes," he said, "I guess I'm sick. Where d'you want to go—back to Lefevre's or home?"

"Home—if you're sick. But ain't it the rotten luck that we've got to miss what the boys will be saying? Come on, then! Is the booze getting to you? Don't you worry about nothing; I'll take care of you. Turn to your right. Here we are!"

He stopped at the door of her rooming house. "Good night," he said. "It was a fine party."

She caught his arm. "You seen some one else just now!" And as that made him start, panic swept her away at the thought of losing this gold mine.

"Don't be making a fool of yourself, honey," she said, attempting to fondle him. "That stuff at Lefevre's went to your head, and you don't know what you're doing—if I let you go back to that crowd they'll pick you clean. You'll lose every cent you—"

He drew back a little from her until a dull light from the nearest window fell on his face, and she saw in it enough to make her release his arm with a gasp. Then rage was born from hopelessness.

"Go back, then," she shrilled. "Go back and find some flat-faced booby who'll get out of you all that I didn't get." She slipped into the half-open door, holding it ready to slam in his face. "You pinhead!" cried Alice-of-the-window. "I'd of trimmed you right to your skin in another hour. Go back and find her, and I hope she hooks you for good and keeps you working overtime like the sucker you are!"

Instead of advancing he turned to Moonshine and hooked his arm over the neck of the stallion. They went off together like two friends, and she heard him saying: "It's better to be a hoss than to be a man and born blind, like I am. There ain't nobody as big a fool as I am. Why, I'll be thinking a light in a kitchen is a star in the sky, pretty soon."

"Crazy!" muttered Alice. "Plain nutty!"

She slammed the door. And straightway she burst into tears. "I wish I was dead," sobbed Alice as she dragged herself slowly up the steps, but the vanity case was tight in her grip!

Who can prophesy what our dreams will be? Even an agony of remorse could not keep Lee awake, and when he slept he met, in a bright vision, the girl with Handsome Harry. He saw her leave Harry and come to him. And he took out the glove and tried it on her hand. Behold! Her hand fitted it as the foot of astonished little Cinderella fitted the slipper. Only the pink tip of one finger showed through the torn end.

He wakened in a flood of golden sunshine and in a mood of no less golden happiness that started him laughing softly.

"Well," drawled a voice. "You got cause for laughing, I guess!"

He heaved himself up on one elbow and saw old Billy Sidney tilted back in a chair in the full glare of the sunshine, his hat on the back of his head, and his knife leisurely employed in whittling a stick of soft pine into grotesque shapes. Lee Garrison blinked at him until in swift stages the truth about the night before crowded upon his memory and made him sit up with a groan.

The old man did not turn his head. "That's life for ye," he said at length. "A-laughing one minute and a-groaning the next. Well, well, well!"

"How come you here?" asked Lee, swinging his legs down from the bed and dropping his elbows on his knees. But his question was received with a counter interrogation.

"Is your head a-swelling and a-busting now, maybe?"

asked Billy Sidney tenderly, turning toward the youth.

"No," said Lee.

"Ain't it now?" The busy white eyebrows went up. "Well, hornswoggle me if that ain't queer! Crawford, now, he moans and cusses and shows his teeth when he wakes up of a morning after blotting up red-eye the way you was doing last night. But you're younger. That's it. Oh, they's a pile of gifts that young folks has that they don't know enough to be thankful for."

"Crawford sent you over to ask me to pay up damage done to his dance floor when the hoss pranced on it—is that why you're here, Billy?"

The ancient wagged his head in melancholy dissent. "If spoiled dance floors was all that you owed Crawford," murmured Billy Sidney, "he'd be a happier man than what he is this blessed morning, lad!"

"Then, what else did he lose? I'll pay."

"You'll pay? Then pay the good name that he used to have that's gone now. Bring back the crowds that used to go drink there and that'll never drink in a place of his again. No, sir, never no more will gents hunting a good time go to Crawford's—only them that want cheap liquor, and rotten cheap it is!"

Upon this amazing speech Lee focused his attention in vain. He could make nothing of it, and he said as much to his strange visitor. Billy Sidney turned toward him at last.

"Didn't you show us the rotten yaller heart of Crawford's?" he asked. "Didn't you take the gal back that he'd told to stay out, and didn't you take her on hossback? And then didn't you make him crawl like a hound?"

For every statement his pointing hand jerked up and his voice squeaked higher. He relaxed from this climax and settled back in his chair.

"Yes, Garrison, you done all that, and more. When you left I was plumb sick, thinking of the time that I'd wasted trying to drag Crawford up and make a man of him. I unbuttoned the flap of my holster and got my old gun loose in the leather. I walked up to Crawford and told him plain what I was thinking. I was sure particular to leave nothing out. You'd think he'd of tied me in a knot and throwed me through the window? No, sir, he couldn't take his eyes off of my old hand, wrapped around the butt of my gun, and pretty soon he wets his lips and looks up at me sort of scared, like a kid waiting for the teacher to whip him!

"And that's Crawford—man-eating Crawford—that's all he is: yaller, yaller, yaller! I walked out of his place all holler inside to think that a thing like him should look so much like a man! Out in the air, I took a glimpse at my gun and seen that it wasn't loaded, but it might of been a whole cannon, Garrison, for all of Crawford. No, sir, you couldn't get a starving man to step inside of Crawford's boots today, he's that low!"

"I'm sorry," said Lee. "I'm sure sorry for the poor devil. Did you come down to tell me that story?"

The old man snorted. "I thank heaven," he said, "that I ain't one of them that has to have reasons for everything they do. Sump'n told me that I'd better slide down here early this morning. Down I come, and the lady of the house says that you ain't up. 'It don't make no difference,' says I. 'I'll wait till he wakes up.'

"'Mister,' says she, 'I don't know's I know you.'

"'I don't know as you do,' says I, 'and I'm sorry for you. Kindly step out of the way!'

"Polite but turrible firm. That's me with women folk. Give 'em an inch and they take a mile. I never give 'em that inch of a finger hold to start with. Well, sir, I come in here and what d'you think I seen? I seen you lying there with the sun on your face. Was it spirits that brought me clean the length of the town to put that chair there to keep your eyes shaded? I dunno, but here I been sitting ever since, watching out that nothing happens. I can see that you need a pile of watching, son. Did they break you last night before you finished?"

And Lee Garrison knew that the old fellow had adopted him.

"If they did," he said, "there's plenty more money to be won at Lefevre's."

"No, sir," said Billy. "First thing I'm going to do is to break you of that gambling habit, son."

"You think you could cure me, Billy?"

"If patience will do it," asserted Billy Sidney, "I'm the most outlastingest gent that ever you seen."

"In the meantime," said Lee, "hadn't I better try one more whirl while I'm getting some coin to start on?"

"Money? Money ain't nothing that counts," said the old man. He drew out a wallet and tossed it to Lee. "Use that," he said, "and when it's gone, something else will turn up. Ever notice that nobody starves in this heaven-blessed world of ours?"

Lee raised the worn leather wallet. "This is about all you've got in that same heaven-blessed world, ain't it?"

"Ain't I just been saying that money don't count?" snapped out Billy. "They's five hundred in that. It ain't so much, and it ain't so little if you go easy when you're spending."

Lee tossed the wallet back to the old man's lap. "You got a good heart, Billy," he said, "and you think you've got hold of some wild, man-killing, gold-eating wildcat. But I ain't, Billy. I'm none of them things."

153

The old man gazed upon Lee with gentle eyes.

"This town thinks it knows me, but it don't," argued Lee. "It's all a misunderstanding. I've won some money by blind luck, and most like I'll never win another penny. I don't need nobody to ride herd on me, Billy. I'm not a trouble maker. Will you believe me?"

"Sure I will," said Billy Sidney. "You're a lamb, you are. You're plumb covered with soft fleece, I guess. Yep, they all figure the same way—they all figure that they're flying around like doves of peace."

"Ain't you going to believe me?" cried Lee.

"I believe every word you say, son. Sure I do. I ain't come to ride herd on you. Shucks, no. I'm just here to pass the time of day and keep out any bad men that might come in here and bother a peaceful feller like you and get your nerves shook up!"

Lee lay back on the bed and laughed feebly. With or without his assent, he felt that a partnership had been formed.

22

"TELL me what they've been saying about me today," asked Lee with painful eagerness.

Billy Sidney grinned. "They say you're one of them quiet gents that thinks every day is Sunday," he said.

"Tell me the truth," pleaded Lee.

"Well," admitted Billy, "I had a look at some red eye in that new dump the man from Chicago is opening up."

"They were talking about the fool I made of myself last night, I guess," muttered Lee.

"They was talking about how Crawford left town last

night," chuckled the old man. "Out he slipped before dawn, and whipped his hosses down the valley. But he can't travel so fast and so far that the news of what he is won't come along and catch up with him, the yaller dog! Come to think of it, they was a little talk about you, too. I guess that surprises you, maybe?" And he winked at Lee.

"You got a talent for picking up the news, Billy."

"It ain't a talent; it's a gift," said Billy. "I don't do nothing but sit still and pretty soon gents begin to tell me all about themselves. Just keeping still works better than asking questions."

"But what were they saying?" insisted Lee impatiently.

"They were saying," chuckled Billy with another wink, "that for a gent that don't make a business out of it, you sure got a pile of luck, son! You raked in a lot of admiration, Garrison. And you got Harry Chandler so worked up that he wants to run Laughter agin' Moonshine. About a thousand gents have been going up to Harry and saying that they thought Moonshine was a finer set-up hoss than Laughter, and that he'd just nacherally walk away from the mare if they had a race. But Harry'll be along and talk to you about it, most like. He's a-ramping and a-raving. It's plumb blasphemy to him, this talk that any hoss in the mountains can run faster than Laughter. Would you bet on Moonshine agin' the mare?"

Lee Garrison laughed and waved his hand.

"She's a clean-bred one," cautioned the old man.

But Lee had passed beyond thought of horses. "I seen a girl with Harry last night," he said.

"Can you see Harry when there ain't a girl with him?" asked Billy. "Was it in Lefevre's?"

"It was outside. She was pale and kind of dark-eyed. And she looked sort of young."

"That might fit a dozen," observed Billy Sidney. "I never

seen a camp like this; Gus Tree says that he ain't, either. Gents have brung along wives and daughters like they was going homesteading instead of mining—which it ain't such a bad idea, at that, to have a woman along for cooking, and such, and leave both of a man's hands free for breaking rock. That reminds me—"

"If you ever seen the girl I'm talking about," said Lee thoughtfully, "you wouldn't be saying that they's a pile of others like her, because there ain't. You mind that I don't mean she's the kind that a gent would turn around to stare at when she went by him in the street; but he'd wake up in the middle of the night and see her face plain as though daylight was on it."

Billy Sidney was staring at him with black disapproval, and spelled out the words of his answer with oracular reluctance.

"Maybe the lady you seen," he said, with the word "lady" set off by both pause and emphasis, "maybe the lady you seen, Garrison, was McGuire's girl. Maybe it was Sally McGuire. She's going to marry Harry—of course you know that?"

Lee Garrison rose, crossed the room, and stared out the window. "They'll make an uncommon fine-looking couple," he said.

"They will," said the old man with equal gravity.

"But why ain't there crowds around her?"

"There was until Harry got mixed in, and then they seen there was no chance. Competition don't prosper none around Harry. He's got the looks. And he's a hell-bender in a fight."

"Him!" exclaimed Lee. "He looks more like four-o'clock tea."

"Sure he does. But the reason I been telling you all this, Garrison, is because I knowed he was coming, and I want to warn you. Please don't make no slips when you're chinning with Harry! And he ain't fifty steps down the street right now!"

He was even closer. The words were hardly out of Billy's mouth when big Harry Chandler stood at the open door and nodded a greeting to them.

"If Billy is here," said Harry, "you know the talk that's going around the town, Garrison. They've gone wild over Moonshine. I've had a steady string of men dropping in to bet me that the stallion can beat my mare. They've worn me out, as a matter of fact, so I've come over to see what you think of a race."

"I've never seen the mare," said Lee.

Chandler lighted a cigarette and studied Lee for a moment through a veil of smoke before he answered. "Suppose we take a look at her, then?"

So they crossed the street. Behind the line of houses, in a box stall far more solidly and spaciously built than most of the houses in Crooked Creek, they looked in at Laughter. She was one of those glossy, night-dark browns which a sheen of perspiration turns into glistening black. She came to meet them with pricking ears and nibbled mischievously at the hand which Chandler held out to her.

It was a beautiful head, wide across the brow, bony, small muzzled, and with great dark eyes like the eyes of a deer. Lee Garrison looked on her with delight, then stepped behind the stall with the others. Viewed from the side, she was a new chapter in his knowledge of horses. Long barreled, thin of belly, she had what seemed to Lee an awkward length of leg. For the quick-dodging, twisting work of a round-up she would be worse than useless. How she could carry the weight of Harry through a single day was a mystery.

But there was a reason. Along the sloping shoulders and down the thigh to the hock she was muscled like a greyhound. There was ample bone, too, and plenty of girth where the forward cinch runs, and where size means lung power. Yes, she had strength to spare to drive those spindling legs, but every ounce of her muscle was placed at the point of greatest need.

"If a man was to ask me," said Billy Sidney, "I'd say that her and Moonshine ain't made for the same sort of running. Give her a nice stretch of flat land and not too far to go, and you couldn't catch her if you had a saddle on the wind. But over rough going through the hills Moonshine would break her heart in half an hour. That's my idea."

"No one has asked you for your idea!" said Chandler with violence. "I followed Moonshine for three days on this horse and couldn't lay a rope on him—he made a fool of us."

"Because Moonshine was carrying nothing but his skin, and Laughter had a couple of hundred pounds on her back," mused Lee.

"I understand," said Chandler, leading the way out of the stall. "Your horse is for show purposes, Garrison, not for use?"

Lee winced, for half a dozen men had gathered about them, and others were coming from the distance. To deny Moonshine before the world would be almost like denying his God.

"You've got a sprinter," he said, "and I've got a long-distance horse. If we could fix up a race that would be fair to both of 'em."

"Why," said Harry smoothly, "occasionally stakes are run up to distances as high as two miles and a quarter. What about a two-mile race, Garrison?"

But Lee shook his head. "If it were ten—" he began.

"I've been speaking of a race," broke in Chandler, "not a day's march. Suppose we compromise and make it three miles. That is surely enough for any horse."

GALLOPING DANGER

"That's quite a ways," said some one in the gathering crowd, and there was a murmur of assent. "Moonshine would clean her up in two miles, even," said another. "Ain't you got any faith in your hoss, Garrison?"

"He doesn't like the idea of a race," said Chandler to the crowd.

"Make it four miles," said Lee.

"Ah," exclaimed Harry, "he'll run his horse against Laughter at four miles! Garrison, I accept! We try them out this afternoon in Sheep Valley."

And he held out his hand. Instinctively Lee took it, though the warning voice of "Bad-luck" Billy cried: "Sheep Valley is as level as the palm of your hand. Not there, Garrison!"

"He's shaken hands on it," said Chandler, grinning. "The bargain is made, Billy. Go croak in another place."

And Lee, with despair, turned toward Laughter, where she stood at the door of her stall, watching them with bright eyes. He had been trapped!

"As for the bet to bind the bargain," went on Harry, lighting another cigarette, "name anything you wish. I'll try to cover it; anything up to the skin of Laughter herself."

"Whatever you want," said Lee wretchedly.

"Moonshine against Laughter, then—the winner takes the other horse. Shake again on that, Garrison!"

There was a stir of excitement in the crowd as it thickened. But Lee stepped back.

"Risk the horse on the race? Good heaven, no!"

"I thought of the sky as the limit," said Harry to the spectators. "But, of course, a horse race is not run in Lefevre's."

There was a subdued chuckle. And it maddened Lee. That imp of the perverse which makes us torture the very things we love had him by the throat.

"Moonshine against Laughter, then!" he cried hoarsely. "And there's my hand on it, Chandler!"

There was no chance to retract. He looked down in sick horror at the strong fingers of Chandler clasping his hand.

How he broke through the crowd and regained his room he never could tell, afterward. But there he threw himself face downward on the bunk, covering his eyes with darkness. Like a vain child, he had thrown Moonshine away because he dreaded the scorn of a crowd.

23

FOR a long hour he lay there seeing always that vision of Laughter galloping ahead. When he stood up, Billy Sidney was again sitting in the sun, whittling at the stick—an endless task, for he struck off shavings so thin that the sun gleamed through them as they fell. So deep was the thought of Billy that he did not lift his head as Lee left the room and went out to the corral.

He found it, as usual, with a group of onlookers ranged along the fences; but on this occasion they were not standing in the customary silence, dreaming over the horse. Instead they talked eagerly, with many gestures. From the distance more men were coming in businesslike haste. The first words he heard left no doubt as to the nature of these spectators. Every man there had placed a bet with Harry on the result of the race between Moonshine and Laughter. The news of the duel was spreading as fast as Harry could travel through Crooked Creek, laying his wagers.

"Five hundred of coin I've sweated for," said one, "is on your back, you gray devil."

"I spent two thousand cold trying to catch you, beauty," said another. "Run for me today and win it back!"

A sallow-faced man smoking a cigar came with a notebook in his hand, recording bets. He was making a drive on Laughter, and from the fence he looked over the gray and the gray's owner.

"Tolerable good news you got there, son," he said. "Certainly looks like he could stand up all day. Laying any money?"

"He's betting the hoss!" answered the crowd in an admiring murmur. "He's betting Moonshine on the race!"

The backer of Laughter removed his cigar. "Well, sir," he said, "that's what I call sporting. I'm Henry Dexter, sir." They shook hands. "You got to pardon me if my money and my heart goes with the clean-bred ones, Mr. Garrison. Laughter is a lovely mare, sir, and she carries my coin. But good fortune to you. If your hoss has as much courage as you have, sir, he'll give the mare a race!"

But Lee heard him through a mist. There was only one daylight reality, and that was the beauty of Moonshine. Moonshine, who would wear the saddle of another man tomorrow, and learn in time to raise his head and prick his ears when Harry Chandler spoke!

He went back to the street, and there he met McLeod swinging along with one hand dropped in his coat pocket and the other spinning a cane. He hurried to Lee.

"I can't say that you're wasted in your present profession," he said, "but you might be in advertising, Garrison. You put them asleep at night with your name on every lip, and you waken them in the morning with the same sound. What's this about the race—about Moonshine and Laughter?"

Lee studied the rascal with peculiar interest. That which is wholly evil is often wholly delightful, and in the tumult of dread and wretched expectation which possessed him, it was pleasant to be distracted, even by McLeod.

"A four-mile race?" went on McLeod. "But Laughter is a lightning flash, Garrison. She blows over the ground like a black leaf in the wind. She—why, with training she would be close to a stake horse, Henry Dexter says! And he ought to know. Is it true that you've bet? Have you really gone deep?"

"I've bet Moonshine to win," answered Lee. And he half wished that he could lead the doctor to plunge the same on the lost cause.

"Moonshine to win! That's betting. What's the scheme, Garrison? Well, I've half a mind to follow your lead; but Laughter is a witch!"

"Is Charlie better?" asked Lee.

"Turning the subject, eh?" chuckled McLeod. "But I don't mind. No, Charlie is on his last legs. Guttorm began to see through the fog I've drawn around him. This morning Charlie had a hemorrhage, and Guttorm ran all the way to the far end of town, dragged Doc Larramee out of bed, and made Larramee run all the way back with him. Larramee is a hardy scoundrel. No more care for a man's feelings than for a piece of stone. He spent thirty seconds looking at Charlie. I was sitting in the next room waiting, and I timed him. Then he came out.

" 'What can be done?' says poor Guttorm. 'It's only a little setback? He's coming through all right?'

" 'He'll die before two days,' says Larramee.

"Guttorm let out a cross between a moan and a howl. Then he looked to me. He'd made up his mind, when the hemorrhage came, that I was no good. The minute he heard the truth he turned back to me.

" 'It ain't true, doc?' he says to me.

" 'Certainly not,' says I.

" 'You scoundrel!' bellows Guttorm at Larramee. 'Get out!'

"Larramee is a big man. But Guttorm picked him up by the neck and the seat of the trousers, the way big boys pick up little boys to throw them into the swimming pool. Guttorm threw Larramee through the door in exactly that manner. The doctor hit the ground, splashed a few curses around, and then got up and swore he'd come back with a gun. Guttorm didn't hear. He was back in Charlie's room, stroking the brat's forehead.

" 'Take your hand away,' says Charlie; 'it's rough!'

"Guttorm came out into the next room with me. They'd brought him a couple of pounds of the first gold out of the new strike he made. He grabbed the bag out of his pocket and dropped it into mine.

" 'You're going to stick by us, doc, ain't you?' he said. 'You wouldn't leave me now, just because I flew off the handle, and—'

" 'I'll be with you as long as I can do the slightest good for you, Guttorm,' said I. And he followed me all the way to the street, thanking me with tears in his eyes. By birth and education, Garrison, that Scandinavian is a fool! But to come back to this race. I understand it's at five this afternoon. Shall I back Moonshine?"

"As you please," said Lee quietly.

"Will any one else in town bet on your horse, though, against a flash like Laughter?"

"Every one who ever tried to run Moonshine down with a string of horses, and there seem to be plenty of them here."

The doctor paused, spun his cane while he frowned at the ground, and then with a curt farewell was off down the

163

street. Whatever his plans were, he was in haste to put them into execution. Lee looked after him with profound envy. If conscience is man's most mortal disease, the doctor was immune to the plague.

A rider halted beside him with the dust spurting under the feet of his horse. "You're Lee Garrison, ain't you?" he asked.

"Yes."

"Miss McGuire wants to know can she see you?"

He had felt that there was nothing in the world which could make him forget Moonshine and his melancholy, but this name in the instant brushed the clouds from the sky and let the kind sunshine fall upon him.

"Sally McGuire? She wants to see me?"

"She does. I dunno——" The messenger clamped his teeth on the rest of the sentence and twitched his cow pony around.

"Wait a minute, partner. Where's she now?"

"The brown tent to your left, just outside of town."

Scratching for the start, the cow pony cast up a great fog of dust, and then drew away at a rapid gallop, while Lee headed for the store. There he purchased a shirt of blue China silk and a new scarlet bandanna, which, when the knot was turned under his chin, left a tip that flowed halfway down his back.

These touches, he felt, made him presentable, but he stepped hastily into the street with an uncomfortable impression that he had kept her waiting long—far too long. He looked up at a sound of merriment, and in the upper story of the hotel, crowded into the narrow frame of a window, he saw Alice and another girl.

When he paused, their laughter pealed again. No doubt she was rehearsing the story of how she had trimmed him.

But the mockery could not harm him now. He stared up to her with an impersonal interest. Merciful shadows of evening and cunning art of the make-up, how terribly they were needed now! But it seemed to Lee that he was seeing her not so much in the glare of the morning as in the light of Sally McGuire.

He raised his sombrero to them—an act which strangely silenced their mirth—and walked on.

24

IT was the most sumptuous and houselike tent that Lee had ever seen. The furled sides exposed an interior so luxurious that he felt it was worthy of being put under glass. Even the ditch which had been trenched around the outside of the tent was set off with borders of little white stones, all of a size. Lee was filled with awe.

A sound of hammering led him around to the side of the tent. There he saw Sally McGuire driving a tent peg in deeper with a mallet. She swung it with wonderful grace, he thought. The wind curled the khaki dress about her, and there was a supple play in that lithe body from the waist to the strong, small wrists. It was a matter of secondary consideration that the mallet twisted awry in her hands and landed first on one side of the peg and then on the other, loosening it far more rapidly than it was driven into the earth.

"If you'd lemme help—" began Lee.

She whirled on him, red of face. The vibrations of the pounding had shaken her hair loose, so that a strand of it coiled halfway down her cheek, and other strands were plastered to her forehead with perspiration. The wide felt hat which protected her from the sun sat crookedly upon her head. And even the red tie which girt the collar of her blouse was shifted far to the side. Smiles, to be sure, will redeem much, but the vexation which a pretty girl feels when fate exposes her in disarray left Sally McGuire in what can only be described as a staring rage. Such a mood as causes children to break their toys now made Sally McGuire fling the mallet upon the ground.

And Lee was utterly bewildered. How could he recognize the pale-faced beauty of the evening before? But if an illusion of mystery were lost, who will not exchange the unapproachable beauty of a dream for daylight flesh and blood not altogether different from other girls? In the meantime, a few swift ministrations of her fingers and the stray threads of hair were tucked away, the hat and necktie righted. A great effort conjured the smile of polite greeting to her lips, but her eyes remained dark—there was a stinging blister raised by that infernal mallet on her right hand!

"You sent for me," said Lee.

"Yes," she answered. "Thank you for coming. And if you don't put your hat on you'll get sunstroke."

He placed it on his head in haste. Of a surety this was not the sad-eyed girl of the night before! He was led inside the tent and a folding stool pointed out. There he sat with his hat in his hands between his knees, desperately conscious that his hair was blown on end and wagging in the breeze. She sat just opposite, erect, her hands dropped in her lap, her eyes inescapably direct. Lee recognized the awe which spread over him; many a time in his childhood he had felt it when the schoolteacher turned on him and he had chilly foreknowledge that he was about to be called on for an answer he did not know. Girls did not wear guns, decided Lee, because they did not need them.

"It's about the horse race," she said, "your Moonshine against Laughter." She paused, drew a little breath, and went on: "I understand that Laughter ought to win, but that there is a chance that she may fail." It began to dawn on Lee that her crispness was an unnatural manner, and that, as a matter of fact, she was badly frightened. "In fact, I understand you're so sure of winning that you've bet your horse!"

"I made that bet—yes."

"Very good," said she. "Now, the point is, Mr. Garrison, that for lots and lots of reasons Moonshine mustn't win, and I'll pay to see that he loses!"

She drew out a check book and a pen. "How much does this race mean to you, Mr. Garrison? Why I have courage to talk so frankly is simply because I understand that you make a business out of—chance, you know."

"They've told you I'm a gambler?"

"I know," she said with a faint smile. "You have to deny it, as a rule. But here is a time when you need not pretend. Not the least bit. I just want to finish this as quickly as I can. So tell me frankly, Mr. Garrison, how much does this race mean to you in dollars and cents. Count in the price of the horse and all your bets—I won't argue about the amount as long as it's in reason."

With how neat an accuracy she laid the last of her contempt upon him. He was a gambler; therefore his very soul was for sale!

"Other men are betting on my horse," he said.

"Other men can take their chances. Besides, I'd pay back what they lose."

"You're doing this for Chandler?"

"I'm asking you to name the amount, Mr. Garrison." It was consummate torture to sit so close to her contempt. But did she realize the full baseness of the thing she asked him to do?

"If Moonshine is winning," he said, "you want me to pull him up and cheat the men who risked their money on him and me? And cheat Moonshine, too, when he's fighting to win!"

She fired up at that. "But if Laughter is beaten, the man who owns her will be beaten, too. And one more blow will break him—oh—I know it! He isn't made to struggle for money. One more blow will crush him. What do I care for small points of honor? I'm fighting to save the soul of a man, and I'll do it!"

And he remembered those far-off days when he had struggled down the trail, footsore, heartsick, and seen the beauty of Moonshine on a hilltop above and beyond him. "Do you know how I got my horse?" he asked.

She shook her head.

"I walked a thousand miles through the mountains, across five States."

"You walked?" she cried, amazed.

"I was sitting in a dugout down in the staked plains reading 'Malory.' Do you know that book?"

Her eyes were parted with her wonder as she nodded.

"Well, into my dugout came a man that might of stepped right out of a book. It was an Indian. And he'd worn himself to death on the trail of a horse just the way the knights died for the Grail. And I listened to him raving about Moonshine; I saw him die. And when I buried him—there was Moonshine cutting across the hills, looking like he was made out of light! Oh, but he was glorious!"

He stopped as that picture burned home in his mind. "I started after him the way I was, on foot; I kept on walking till my feet cut to pieces. I trailed him up into the mountains where I near froze. I trailed him down to the lava where I near died of thirst. I crossed the Colorado. I kept on going till my ammunition was gone. And after it was gone I threw away my gun and lived on the sage hens and the grouse I could knock over with sticks and stones. I got thin and shriveled up with starving and no sleep. My hand was like the hand of an old man. But always Moonshine was galloping away ahead of me like there was wings on his feet, and it seemed to me if I could catch him I'd die happy.

"And sometimes I got into a rage. I wanted to ride him to death. I wanted to make him know that he had a master. And always he was getting thinner and weaker, until finally I managed to rope him.

"He was too weak to buck me off when I let him up. But off in the hills he heard a waterfall hollering like a hundred men, and the noise blowing away to a whisper and coming back with a shout. He couldn't get me off any other way, so he ran for that waterfall to kill himself—and stay free! I seen what he was aiming at, but I stayed on. Seemed to me it was better to die fighting him than to give up. We jumped the cliff together and landed in the water underneath. I wasn't hurt, but one of his hoofs was torn loose, and he was stunned.

"Well, I dragged him on shore, dammed the water away, and tied up the hoof with mud and bark. There I stayed week after week waiting for the hoof to get well, wondering if it would heal so's he could walk on it, and all the time getting thicker and thicker with that hoss. I pulled up grass to feed him. I built a shelter over him. And all those weeks I was happy. He got so's he could hobble around on three feet, with the bad foot held up in a sling from hitting the ground, and him that I'd hated and trailed that thousand miles—he'd come to me when I whistled; he'd come to me when I called!"

He threw back his head with his eyes closed, trembling with the joy of that great time.

"He'd eat from my hand; he'd lie down at my feet; he'd follow me like a friend. Then the great day came. I took the sling off and let his foot touch the ground. Would he be able to walk, or was he lame for life? I couldn't bare to look to see. I closed my eyes."

Lee shuddered with the horror of it. "Then I heard him begin to trot away, and he was hobbling just on three feet. He was ruined forever, I thought, and it made me sick. I ain't a praying man, but I lifted up my head with my eyes still shut and begged God to help him. And a minute later I heard Moonshine galloping—galloping with all four hoofs striking the ground, and I knew I'd won—I knew I'd won.

"We started on, with me on his back. His strength and his speed came back. He was like a king, but when I spoke to him he went slow or fast as I told him, and when I touched his neck he'd turn.

"Then, one day, we came on a wild herd, and Moonshine went mad at the sight of them. And it seemed to me it was better to lose him forever, if he wanted to go, than to keep him with me when half of his heart all the rest of his life would be aching to be off running with the band he'd been king of. So I got off him. I told him to go! And he went like the wind."

"Oh, no, no!" breathed the girl.

"But he came back!" cried Lee, throwing out his hands in exultation. "He came back to me, and when Moonshine found I wouldn't go with him, he went on with me."

He called himself back from the story. He saw her face again, and there were great tears in her eyes.

"You see," he said gently, "that's why it's hard to give him up. I simply couldn't give him up."

"Oh," she said, "what a beautiful story! I didn't know— how could I dream—" She bit her lip, as though one part of her sentence would be better unspoken. She dropped her face in her hands, lost in thought.

"But, after all," she said when she looked up, "you'll only lose Moonshine for a few days. There is no reason why I should keep the secret. I am to marry Harry Chandler, and after we are married I can persuade him to give back your horse. It's only a question of telling him the story you have told me."

Lee shook his head. "Nobody could give up Moonshine," he said.

"But I promise! Oh, Harry is the soul of generosity and honor. That's the very thing which has spoiled all his chances. There's no germ of the money-maker in him, and he's sworn he will not marry me until he can support me without my fortune. But money is nothing to me. My father has made ten fortunes and piled them one on another. My mother made me rich in my own name. It means nothing to give you whatever the loss of this race can be worth to you. But while it means nothing to me, it is everything to Harry. Today he's taking his last chance. If he fails—he'll ride out of my life and into some wild adventure—I know—I know!"

There was no more storm and defiance. She had clasped her hands together in entreaty, and Lee could no longer resist that tugging at his heartstrings. He stood up.

"Then Moonshine will lose," he said. "I'll give my word!"

"God bless you!" cried Sally McGuire. "And now the money—"

"I'll manage that, someway."

"But I can't take charity, you see."

171

She blocked his escape. "Mr. Garrison! What are you going to do?"

"What I've given you my word I'll do."

"But—"

"Will you do one favor for me?"

"Yes, yes—and the check will be whatever—"

"Will you try on this glove?"

He drew out the old, tattered glove which he had carried so far, and she, bewildered, slipped her hand into it. It fitted to a minute perfection and, just as he had imagined, the rosy tip of a finger projected through the torn end.

"What does it mean?" asked Sally McGuire, as she stripped it off and returned it to him.

It seemed to Lee that emotion would choke him. Fate, then, must have taken a hand and guided him from the shanty among the mountains to the girl who had lived in it.

"It means nothing," stammered Lee, and took advantage of her wonder to slip past her, through the doorway, and into the night.

25

THE uproar from the mines was ending as he left, token that Crooked Creek was already leaving the mines to gather for the race.

The sunshine was neither bright nor warm as he went down the street again, and he noted the increased length of the shadows which meant that the time for his parting with Moonshine was not far off. He turned to glance back at the tent, but she was not standing at the entrance to call him back and restore his promise. Instead, his eye glanced on to that mountain capped with white rock now thrusting so high into the tender blue of heaven. A curse had fallen upon him from that landmark toward which so many others were hurrying, even now, as the goal of hope!

He shut himself up in his room for an hour. Even Billy Sidney could not come. It was not until the time for the race was close at hand that he went out again. He found a crowd around the corral. Little Gus Tree stepped out to meet him.

"Well," he chuckled, "I see that you ain't on your way for the mines, yet? You ain't started with a drill and a single-jack, son?" Coming a bit closer, he jerked his thumb over his shoulder in the direction of Moonshine. "Shall I get money down on him, son? Don't seem to me like he has the legs to stand off that Laughter here. But I ain't a hoss-flesh expert. You tell me what to think, will you, Garrison, and I'll do my talking in hard cash."

"You may be rich," said Lee bitterly, "but you'd have to be terrible rich to afford to bet on Moonshine."

"Unless the weight of Harry breaks Laughter down?"

"That won't happen, I guess."

"Then why in the devil are you racing against—" The barber stepped away, shaking his head solemnly. "I dunno how you figure this, Garrison. You're certainly deep!"

Lee pressed by him until he heard the voice of Billy Sidney and saw that ancient worthy in an attitude of commanding importance.

"No other hoss in the world," Billy was saying, "would of lived through the busting that this hoss took. But they's only one Moonshine. Put your money where you please, boys, but when Garrison finished betting Moonshine against Laughter, he turns around to me and says: 'Billy, was there anything easier than that, ever? But it's a shame to take his mare away from—' Here he is now, Lee!"

The unblushing old liar turned with a smile and a wave toward his newfound patron.

He saddled by a mechanical effort and led Moonshine out through the gate and swung onto his back. After that the crowd which had started for Sheep Valley carried them along. Passing the hotel, he looked up and saw Alice at the window with the sun on her face. She pointed to herself and then back to him, and at last brandished a handful of greenbacks—a sign language to say that she had wagered heavily on his good fortune. Then she hung out the window, kissing her hand to him.

How could she smile on him today, he wondered vaguely, when last night was such a short distance behind them? But she and the yellowing sunshine and the faces it glinted upon and the rolling of voices were dreamy things which he saw as a child sees when it is tired. So he and his followers came out below the town and into the open where the hills pushed back. To the right Crooked Creek hummed and talked to one side and twisted its muddy waters down the slope. But the drift of people—and every one from the mines had gathered before them or was hastening now from the rear—set in toward a flat table-land of sandy ground, the partially filled floor of the valley from which the river had disappeared long centuries before. But it wound back now as a river valley will, the white sand turning to brown and to blue in the distance where the valley disappeared. The populace of Crooked Creek had bunched at the mouth of the plain, in the greater part, for the start and the finish could be best seen there. But others, willing to miss the two most exciting instants for the sake of seeing a greater portion of the race from a good angle, had spread thin lines which, with many a gap, roughly sketched the four-mile loop of the course, and their forms dwindled in distance, at the far end, more obscured by a haze of dust which a wind of gathering force blew up the valley.

So much Lee saw before his attention focused on Laughter. She was full sixteen three, and the more exaggerated in apparent height by the size of the boy in the saddle. There was no need of Chandler standing at the head of the brown mare to identify it. There could not be two of that kind—this was invincible Laughter!

And what a heart-stopping beauty as she danced and tossed her head, played with the bit, shrank back and winced to the side, and then pawed a cloud of dust into the air, and jerked her nervous head about to watch it jerked into nothingness by the whip of the wind.

No wonder Harry had wagered his last dollar on her, for she was framed and molded to one and only—speed! She pranced about and faced Lee. It was a knife edge that she presented to the wind of her gallop. There was lung space enough where the girths ran, but her chest was not so broad as to interfere with the long, elastic sweep of the shoulders. Her neck was straight as a string, and her head on the eye of it was snaky thin. How different from the haughty and arched crest of the stallion! Now Harry loosed her head and off she went, going out into a long, rolling gallop. Lee Garrison watched her shoot past the watchers.

They gave her an excited shout of admiration as her diminutive rider brought her up and turned her back—she was clumsy and sprawling in that turn, Lee thought. Then he saw the face of the boy who was exercising her. It was Buddy Slocum!

In the meantime those who had gathered in wait saw the gray champion coming, and they raised a cheer which showed in a thrice where their hearts lay. The horse they valued truly was one which they knew could answer the test

GALLOPING DANGER

of the desert and mountain and fierce labor day by day under a withering sun that would kill Laughter between sunrise and sunset. There were cow-punchers, also, who might gasp in admiration at the enormous bounds of the mare, but who, thinking of the short stops, the twists and turnings of the round-up, the foot-handiness which a horse must have to be worth his salt, shook their heads when they saw the tall black sprawling as she turned. For them, and for all who had ridden the grisly trail from sea-level desert to timber-line snow, Moonshine was the horse. A full hand shorter than Laughter, he had twice her strength in his sturdy quarters and in the rubbery cords of muscle which slipped and bunched along his shoulders. That gaunt belly of hers would tuck up to famine leanness in a day or two, and the greyhound back would buckle under a crushing burden, whereas Moonshine, with a fine long line below that promised speed enough, had the shortness above that meant strength. He would gallop all day with a quarter of a thousand pounds.

The confidence of the stallion's supporters grew. They shouted affectionate encouragement to him. A reckless miner ventured too close, and the heels of the stallion flashed and bit the hand which the man threw up to shield his face. He fell flat on his back and rolled to safety in a roar of applause. In the eyes of that crowd, Moonshine could do no harm. They blamed him no more than they would have blamed a captive eagle. No matter where their money lay, he was champion of their hearts of hearts.

"Start the race," said old Billy Sidney feverishly. "It's ten minutes to five already, and Moonshine is running a mile every minute you wait!"

Behind the fence of the corral Moonshine had endured the nearness of men well enough, for that fence was a symbol that none could approach him, saving the master.

176

But here in the open there could be seen nothing between him and their hands, which moved with fire, and their mouths, which puffed forth smoke like the nostrils of a hungry bear on a frosty morning. Moreover, their nearness made his heart go out suddenly to the freedom of the wide sands before him. As Lee swung down to the ground he crowded closer against the back of the master, keeping his head high, with his upper lip thrust out stiff, and his frightened eyes glittering. He shrank and trembled at the raising of every hand, the sound of every voice.

Compared with this horror of men which set the gray dripping with perspiration, the nervous eagerness of the mare was statuesque calm.

Lee turned from a glance at his horse to Harry Chandler. Between the moment the bet was laid and five o'clock Harry had spent the equivalent of two sleepless nights; he had the same battered look, and the eyes which he lowered toward his cigarette were circled with purple.

"With Slocum in the saddle," said some one, "Laughter looks good enough to beat the wind; but she'll size up a lot different when you fit into the stirrups, Chandler. That's what we're counting on!"

"You are?" asked Harry, and, glancing around the circle at the nodding heads, he exclaimed with a vicious pleasure: "Who said that the owners were to ride? Was that laid down in the conditions? No! Buddy Slocum rides Laughter today!"

26

NEVER did orator, pausing in declamation to receive applause, fall into an attitude more carefully studied than that of the ex-jockey. Before the surprising announcement of Harry had brought attention to quick focus on his champion, little Buddy Slocum had stiffened in the saddle, and now he sat with his arms folded and his chin high and the long visor of his hat shadowing his face down to the joyous grin. Thousands of dollars had been wagered on Moonshine. Now in a breath, hope was snatched from the backers of the stallion. The excitement which had frothed and bubbled in Crooked Creek for half a day expired in a murmured groan from half the crowd and a buzz of contented comment from the rest. Tricks were not popular, nevertheless, and this underhand maneuver brought solemn glances in the direction of Harry.

As for Lee Garrison, the sight of Slocum in the saddle meant that there would be excuse for the defeat of Moonshine. The honor of the stallion would be saved. But, oh, to mate this treacherous move on the part of Harry Chandler by a mighty effort of his own—by a ride which would fairly lift the gray horse over the ground! But his hands were chained. In the meantime there was a frantic clamor from those who had bet on Moonshine and now wished to change and cover their money. In ten seconds there were odds of three to one being freely offered on Laughter, and no Moonshine money in sight! The whole crowd was in a hubbub. Harry Chandler defended himself as well as he could.

"There are plenty of other lightweights," he said. "I don't care who put you up, Garrison, darned if I do! There's Charlie Morton's kid. He doesn't weigh over a hundred and twenty pounds if he's an ounce. Get him!"

There was no need for Lee to answer. A dozen stern voices told Harry what he must already know: That Lee Garrison was the only man whose life was worth a penny on the back of the mustang. That murmur brought dark blood into the cheek of Chandler. He had lived so long in the public eye and with public applause that this sound was poison in his ear, and his impulsive start told Lee that the big man was on the verge of taking the saddle himself. But he checked that impulse; there was too much at stake.

"All right," called Billy Sidney, "if everything's settled, let's start the race. Moonshine is fair wearing himself out. He ain't used to crowds like this, Chandler."

Harry looked again at the sweat-darkened body of the gray and set his jaw. He slipped his watch into his open palm.

"The race was set for five o'clock," he announced, "and it'll be run off at that time—no sooner! If your horse can't stand a crowd you should have kept him away from it."

It was such bad sportsmanship that the men kept quiet in wonder. There was only one sharp, faint exclamation, and Chandler turned to confront Sally McGuire. The women of Crooked Creek had come in their gayest finery, flowerlike in the crowd of miners. How and why they should have brought such clothes into the mountains, no one saving another woman could tell. Sally McGuire was as drab as any breaker of rock in her short skirt and mannish blouse, but the colors of flowers indeed were in her face!

"Shame!" she had cried. "Shame!"

"It's the rules of the race!" exclaimed Harry. "Besides, why shouldn't I take advantage if I can? There's too much up on this race. Good heavens, Sally, you know what—" He checked himself, for she was looking at him in startled amazement.

"She's true blue," breathed Lee to himself. "She's as square as they come. And maybe—pray heaven—she'll learn to look through Harry today. Maybe this race'll show her! Can't anybody see what he is? Just spoiled kid growed into a man!"

Harry Chandler deliberately turned his back on her, bracing his feet wide apart as though prepared to go counter to the opinion of the entire world. It was not a pretty exhibition, and old Gus Tree, removing his hat and polishing his bald head with a purple silk handkerchief, communicated that fact to Harry with his accustomed bluntness.

"I've bet on your hoss, Chandler," he said, "but it sure won't give me no satisfaction if I win."

Harry glowered in the direction of the speaker but before he could directly answer, Gus was calling to men whom he spotted in the crowd: "Hey, Jerry, bets off if you want!" "I sure do, Gus. I wasn't figuring on anything like this." "Hello, Joe—we'll call our bet quits, too."

That fearless denunciation brought up the silenced chorus, and the others began to say what they thought, though it was by no means all of a piece with the speech of Gus Tree. There was too much money wagered on the black mare and though a few imitated the generous example of the barber, the greater majority were loud in defense of the bets they had laid.

It was then that Lee called Billy Sidney to him. "Start betting in my name," he said. "They'll take your bets. Keep going until you've got down fifteen thousand on Moonshine."

"Are you plumb crazy?" groaned poor Billy.

"Do what I tell you. I have a reason?" And a good reason it was, for when Moonshine was beaten, he was resolved that his wallet should be empty.

Across the trembling withers of the stallion he found Sally McGuire watching him with wonder, with doubt, and with sympathy. He took off his sombrero and smiled at her. That act of grace made her crimson to the eyes.

In another moment he saw that the sheriff, watch in hand, had taken his post at one side of the starting line, which had been made by the simple expedient of dragging a heel through the sand. The mare danced up to her place, and Lee, swinging into the saddle, sent Moonshine gliding after. Side by side, the dancing mare and the crouching gray; the contrasts of height and build were more apparent than ever. Despite his diminutive build, Buddy Slocum's eyes were above the level of Lee's. And big Harry Chandler, at the side of his jockey, tucking in the straps of the shortened stirrups, was commanding eagerly: "Send her out right at the start, Buddy. You hear?"

"Sure," said Buddy, "I'll run the gray sick in the first quarter, and after that we'll walk in anyway we feel like coming. You leave it to me, boss! I want his blood."

Lee Garrison leaned over and ran his finger tips down the wet neck of Moonshine. How cruelly unfair it was that the king of the wild horses should be thus tricked into defeat! And by this long-legged racer, unmeant for real use!

Here the voice of the sheriff reached him, a voice pitched high to cut through the rising moan of the wind.

"You head down for them black rocks, three of 'em all bunched together. You circle around them and come back here. Now get your horses on the line. I ain't going to get you prepared. I'm just going to shoot off my gun, and that's a sign for you to let 'er go!"

Deftly little Buddy Slocum, pitched well forward and high above the saddle, with his hands stretched out on the reins, gathered the mare under him, and by the very touch of his fingers seemed to tell her what he expected her to do. His lean face wrinkled in a smile of expectancy for the wind of the gallop, and he rolled the whites of his eyes at Lee with venomous satisfaction.

"You ain't shooting craps now, Garrison! Talking to the dice ain't going to help you. You're going to eat dust, cap—you're going to eat my dust! Steady, lady! Easy, girl!"

By a miracle of control he was keeping the hind feet of the black bunched well forward under her, ready for the leap.

"Keep quiet, folks, will you?" requested the sheriff. Mortal silence spread among the spectators, and no sooner was it established than the gun exploded and sent a mighty forty-five caliber into the sand.

That noise, like a thrust of spurs, sent both horses away from the mark, but in a far different manner. Long trained for a sprinting start, Laughter, with quarters sinking as she dug in her heels, shot away with great bounds, then steadied into a long-sweeping gallop, but Moonshine, away like a ball bouncing off a stone, no sooner felt his head given him than he slackened his pace abruptly, tossed up his head, and made sure that the crowd was not pouring in pursuit. The slap of Lee's hand against his flank and the call of the master at his ear thrust him away again at a racing gait, but the momentary faltering had given the black a vital advantage.

A straight line from head to the tip of her scanty tail, she flew into the lead, with even her ears flattened as though the wind of her going were too great to prick them against it. Low along her neck crouched Buddy Slocum, so glued to her that she cut the wind for her rider as well as herself. Moonshine, straightened out for his full effort, seemed going twice as fast, but ever that long, bounding stride floated the mare farther and farther away. The clamor was all from the supporters of Laughter; from the backers of Moonshine came only one deep shout of dismay. And the faces past which Lee was driving were blank with incredulity.

His own heart was sinking like a stone. How futile the stretch and stride of the gray compared with that reaching gait of Laughter! Would she canter across the finish line, eight or nine minutes later, with Moonshine a quarter of a mile behind? The shame of it made him weak.

Meantime Moonshine, unurged, had caught the spirit of the thing. No doubt when he led a herd some fleet-footed horse had often challenged with speed against speed. Now, as sail after sail is thrown to the wind and the ship gathers headway, so in the deep of his heart the gray was finding strength and greater strength to overtake the flying mare. By jerks his rate increased. Partly for that reason he began to keep even with the pace of Laughter, but there was a greater cause. Buddy Slocum had looked back, and the moment he saw the gap between him and the gray, began to tug at the reins and sit down in the saddle. No doubts remained in the jockey's heart as to the issue of the race; no doubts were in the minds of the gloomy men along the course; no doubts were with Lee Garrison. The breeze was quickening to a gale. The air was a rosy haze as the dust increased. If only the blast would grow to the dark of a sand storm and thus mercifully veil the defeat!

But now, as Moonshine drifted to within three lengths of the mare, Buddy Slocum twisted around and shouted: "I'm going to make it *look* like a race. You can thank me, Garrison!"

His woman-sharp laughter flew back. Lee gritted his teeth and bent lower. Moonshine was flying at the very top of his speed, but Laughter held him even with consummate ease despite a sharp pull. Wear her down? They had covered the first mile of the course, and she was fresh as a daisy, wild for the running.

Half a mile away were the three black rocks. Straight as a string ran the stallion, and Lee knew that he could maintain that gait for miles and miles, unfaltering. But there would be no such demand as that. The run was nearly half covered, and Laughter was fighting for her head!

Now they were at the rocks. Her jockey took her wide, but generous as the loop was on which he guided her, the long-legged mare lost headway and broke her gait, while Moonshine, darting up on the inside, doubled around the rocks like a jack-rabbit. He faced the wind a length in the lead. And what a wind it was! Even going before it, Lee had felt it fanning his back. When they faced it, it struck them heavily. Compressed in Sheep Valley like water narrowing in a flume, the breeze had strengthened to a gale, and now the speed of a running horse was added to it.

Lee Garrison set his teeth in grim satisfaction as Moonshine shook his head at the blast, then pricked his ears. But the spindle-legged mare, designed by generations of careful breeding for speed on a track or over smooth meadows— how would she stand the test?

Glancing back, Lee saw the mare coming like a bullet. She had her head, now, and presently she forced swiftly by him with the ugly face of Buddy Slocum turned toward him with a mocking grim.

Little by little the mare drew clear. She was seventy yards away with only the last mile of the race before them.

And yet with unhesitant courage he still poured every scruple of energy into his work. Those at the finish line could see that the black led, but they could not see by how far, and over their heads the sombreros danced and swung as they cheered on their favorites. Lee could see tall figures thrust up where one climbed on the shoulders of his companions for a clearer estimate.

To finish thirty lengths behind, there was disgrace for which no difference in weight could account! Those scattering outposts who had advanced this far down the course to watch the running of the middle of the race were either slapping one another upon the back and laughing uproariously, or else they were stunned and silent.

In dreary amazement Lee studied the tall black, but it seemed to him that she no longer swept along with the same frictionless stride that had carried ground so easily during the first three miles of the running. She was throwing her forelegs a trifle out of line, as though she had begun to pound a little. Presently she stumbled heavily, slowed, and was thrust onto the bit again by a smart blow of Slocum's whip. He was not keeping that tight rein to hold her in; he was merely riding her as she was accustomed to being ridden, not with the free head and the long rein of a cow pony, but well in hand every instant to keep her straight at full speed, and hold her up when she tired. And she was tiring now. A stumble to a fresh horse is a spur that makes it dart away at redoubled speed as though to leave the shame behind; but a tired horse takes advantage of any interruption to slacken efforts. Not that Laughter was by any means spent. Her faltering was the thing of an instant. Lee Garrison, far in the rear, barely noticed it, but he saw enough to make him guess the rest, and he called on Moonshine with a great voice.

And there was an answer. In that great heart of Moonshine there was still an untapped reservoir of strength. The mare no longer drew away. She was held even; she began to come back. For that weary pressure of the wind was telling heavily. And Lee, riding not to win, but only to save the honor of his horse, stiffened in the saddle and yelled like an Indian on the warpath.

Buddy Slocum jerked around to look, and in that moment he let Laughter flounder into half a dozen strides of sand fetlock deep. The soft going cut her speed in two. She struck the soft ground as though she had run into a wall, and came laboring onto firm going again. She had still a twenty-length lead, and the finish was a scant half mile away, but Buddy Slocum, feeling the tall mare labor and pound, and maddened by the cut of the wind against his face, lost his head.

He snatched out his whip and went after her. She had been running confidently, rejoicing in her work as a good horse should, but now she saw the stallion gaining and felt the man who rode her go into a panic. Instead of the even pressure on the reins, reassuring her, there was a series of jerks and that whizzing whip seared her flanks. The panic of the rider ran into the horse. She bolted in a frenzy for two hundred yards, and then began to stop as though crushing weights had been added to her burden.

Yet she could not lose! The finish was a scant half mile away, and twenty lengths behind came the gray; yet even a tyro now could mark the laboring gallop of the black. And Moonshine, in effort after effort, unwhipped and unspurred, increased his speed. He could tell that he gained even as Lee could tell, and the knowledge was to them as wine to the weary.

And the head of Laughter was coming up—she was spent indeed! Not that she gave up. No, the advantage she held was too great for that, and if her heart was breaking she was uplifted by the creed of an ancient ancestry which died, but never surrendered. No need of the cruel whip or the spurs which were goring her flanks to crimson. She was pouring out the last scruple of her strength, and still, five hundred yards from the end, she led by fifteen lengths by forty mortal yards.

It was enough to have settled all but one race in a thousand, but the men of Crooked Creek seemed to feel that this was perhaps the thousandth event, and were transformed, one and all, into rioting wildmen. And every shout, it seemed to Lee, was a fresh source of energy that helped Moonshine on. He himself was stammering, groaning, at the ear of the stallion. The sands washed dizzily beneath them; it seemed almost that the earth whirled and carried them back, when he looked down. But here was Laughter borne back and back with shortening stride and head jerking.

A furlong away the rioting of the crowd grew less and less. Man after man was frozen into position by the agony of suspense. Some crouched and stretched out their arms with contorted faces. Some were turned to stone in the midst of cheer or groan, and as the deep shouting of the men fell away it was possible to hear the shrilling of the women more distinctly. Only a furlong away the sheriff was cursing the crowd back to clear the finish line, and now gallant Moonshine stretched his nose within four lengths of the blowing tail of the mare.

He was weary, and he had done enough for honor. So long as he lived and that race was spoken of, every man would tell how the impost of extra weight had beaten him—never the speed of Laughter. Then it was that, at the side of the mob, Lee saw Sally McGuire with her hands clasped, her form bowed in the pain of waiting. He must draw rein. Slowly, with a breaking heart, he began to pull back, while under the pressure he felt a shudder go through the gray—but mute testimony that the harmony of effort between them was broken.

Some one was shrieking hoarsely from the side "Moonshine! Moonshine!" It was Billy Sidney, fallen on his knees, with his bony fists brandished in the air. Such a frenzy came on Lee Garrison as had swept him away when the gray turned toward the roar of the waterfall, that day so long ago.

In an instant he was helping the stallion toward the line, and at every jump they gained. Rapidly the empty daylight between them was eaten away. Fifty yards away was the crowd, and men were turning their backs rather than see the inevitable. But it was not inevitable. The heart of Moonshine was deep as a well, and to the very bottom it was filled with clear courage.

His nose was on her hip. It slipped on to her girth. Surely, enough had been done for the honor of Moonshine now! And Lee tightened the reins again and relaxed. And Moonshine relaxed beneath him. The race was lost!

But how could Buddy Slocum tell that when he saw the gray head at the shoulder of his mare? How could he tell that in another stride the stallion would be falling back? He turned a face black with insane rage and fear.

"Damn you!" he shouted, and slashed Moonshine straight across the face with the heavy lash of his whip.

It seemed to Lee Garrison that cowardly blow fell on his own heart. The thought of the girl and the promise was erased from his mind.

"Moonshine!" he shouted, "Moonshine!"

And the good horse had not winced from the blow. He flung himself forward across the line. Lee looked back. The sheriff had raised his sombrero in one hand and his naked revolver in the other. The silence of the crowd was like the silence of a church.

"Moonshine by half a head!" he yelled.

27

AND Moonshine, blackened with sweat, raised a high head with everdistant eyes that seemed to be searching the blue peaks of the distance but which were, in fact, waiting for the voice of the master. The voice did not speak, for Lee had seen Sally McGuire cover her face with her hands and then turn and start slowly back for the town with a gray-headed man beside her.

Yonder stood Laughter, her head low and her legs braced. Buddy Slocum had been torn from the saddle and literally kicked the first hundred feet of the distance back to Crooked Creek. Now Harry Chandler led the mare toward Garrison, and he mechanically dismounted to meet the vanquished. All about them, losers and winners hushed their noise to watch, and Harry met the crisis in the most kingly manner. The excitement brought color to his face. He carried his head high, and even managed to muster a faint smile. Lee Garrison, with bowed head and gloomy face, seemed more the picture of a defeated man. Chandler took his hand and shook it heartily.

"If Laughter had won," he said, "after that scoundrelly trick of Slocum's, I should have given you the race and the horse anyway, Garrison. But here she is! Good luck go with her!"

It was very well done, that speech of congratulation. It was one of those things that sends a chilly prickle down the backs of the bystanders. But Lee, patting the wet forehead of the mare lightly, touched Harry by the arm as he was turning away.

"But I got a hoss," said Lee, "that does for my needs pretty well. Chandler, I can't take her. She's yours."

It was too much for Harry. His nerve crumpled.

"D'you think I take charity, Garrison? Give her away if you don't want her. Feed her to the dogs. I'm through with her!"

And with a contorted face, more maddened by the

knowledge that he had destroyed the effect of his previous acting, he plunged through the mob and was gone. That departure cost only a momentary cloud however. Even the men who had backed Laughter heavily, declared that the race they had seen was worth the money they had lost, and Lee Garrison was escorted back to the town as a conquering hero.

If he were a gambler, at least he seemed a straight one, and of his generosity as victor they had been witnesses. Ten minutes saw him mounted from the trough of suspicion to the crest of popularity. But in that time of victory, as they went slowly back toward the town, with the black mare led behind by half a dozen willing hands, Lee Garrison saw one thing only: Sally McGuire as she bowed her face in her hands and turned away.

In the dark of the evening, when he managed to slip from the crowd, he went straight to his room, with an aching need for solitude. But there he found Billy Sidney waiting like an actor for the rise of the curtain. The old man stood beside the bunk, over which he had thrown his coat. He was smoking a pipe with his thumbs thrust under his suspenders—an attitude of calm weariness with life which was quite gainsaid by the flashing of his eyes.

"Well," he said, "I got the bets down!"

"Good for you, Billy."

"And I brought the winnings in. It ain't much. There's been more coin than this got together here and there. But—here it is, Lee! Here's all there is!"

He jerked the coat away and exposed the top of the heavy bunk groaning under a ponderous mass of gold coin, untarnishable, shimmering yellow. He shoveled from his pockets fresh handfuls which he had kept there for the final effect. Gold showered upon gold with a musical chiming.

"We cleaned up the camp!" shouted Billy Sidney, fairly dancing around the room with joy. "Look at it, Lee! When I started betting I was hollow-hearted. I was sure sick at the thought of backing Moonshine against that long-legged mare with the midget on her back. Right away came a rush of Laughter money. They offered me two to one. I took it in small chunks. It broke me all up to be throwing that gold coin away. But still I kept at it in little bets here and there. When they went up to the start I was getting three to one, and when Laughter went floating away as the race began, I got five to one. I bet a whole thousand with the barber—one thousand agin' five thousand! And I could of gone on betting for ten to one as the race went on, but all the money was gone!"

He could not resist plunging his fingers into the mass as he spoke. As he raised his hands a rain of money clattered down, some falling unheeded on the floor.

Mrs. Samuels, her eyes pressed to the keyhole, nearly fainted at the sight of coined gold underfoot. Had she not been already on her knees she might have fallen. But Lee Garrison had sunk wearily on his bunk.

"Billy," he said, "I want one thing more'n money. I want to be alone."

Billy Sidney loosed with a single crash all the coins which remained in his hands. Then he nodded in admiration. "Still scheming—never satisfied," he said. "Well, that's the way with a genius." And he stole softly through the door.

Now that he was alone, Lee blew out the lamp, but the darkness was no more merciful. He could see her only the more clearly. And he was glad when his door was opened. But it was not Billy Sidney returning; it was the heavy voice of Olie Guttorm which spoke.

"Garrison—are you here?"

191

"I'm here; I'll light the lamp, Olie."

"I don't want no light. I can say what I got to say better in the dark."

He closed the door, and Lee heard a sound of heavy breathing. He fumbled for his revolver and found it. Then he waited again.

The voice of Guttorm began, again, choked away to guttural murmurs, and finally was audible: "Garrison, it's come. I thought that the doctor could save Charlie for me. Did it seem much for a smart man like him to do? I ask you, Garrison?"

"No."

"And McLeod worked hard. He got right down on his knees by the bed and worked hard. But it wasn't no good; Charlie begun to roll his eyes and look every way at once and see nothing. I seen, then, that McLeod couldn't help. Nobody could help. It was the whip for me because of what I done to you. When a man does wrong, he's trying to cheat God.

"I picked up Charlie in my arms and run outside with him where the breathing would be easier. But he kept on gasping. I tried to make a bargain. I called out: 'God Almighty, don't kill Charlie for what I done myself. I'll give Garrison his half. I'll tell that he made the strike.'"

The voice of the prospector swelled to thunder, then fell away.

"It wasn't no good. It was too late to draw back then. Charlie was fighting for his breath. He begun to beat me in the face. I kept telling him to fight hard. But pretty soon he stopped hitting me, and I took him back into the light. All I was holding in my arms was nothing. My Charlie was gone away from me!"

When he could speak again he said slowly: "I went to

Judge Brown. I told him what I owed you, and that half of my mines belonged to you by rights. He done some writing. I signed it, and here it is."

He found Garrison and stuffed the paper into his hand.

"I kept a-hoping, somehow," said Guttorm. "I dunno why. But it seemed after I'd signed that paper that Charlie would come back. He didn't seem no more'n around the corner from me. I run all the way from the judge's shanty to my house. But Charlie's eyes are still closed, and he's still smiling. He ain't going to change."

He drew a great, noisy, sobbing breath, turned with the floor creaking beneath his tread, and went slowly from the house. The front door slammed behind him. The heavy footfalls went up the street, and the rustling of the paper in the dark told Lee that he was rich.

Rich? It meant no more to him than the sound of dead leaves in the wind! It seemed that the smallness of the room crowded the picture of Sally McGuire relentlessly upon him, and at last he went out into the darkness behind the house. Moonshine whinnied plaintively from the corral.

He listened unmoved to that call. Wondering at himself, he felt the dark anger cloud his mind. A day before there would have seemed nothing too great to do for the sake of the wild horse, but now he knew that there is a price on all but one thing in the world, and the price of Moonshine had been exceeded. That beautiful, strong body which the starlight now glimmered over was still his; and the scorn and the hatred of Sally were his also!

Yet automatically he went on to the fence of the corral. He had formed the habit of going near Moonshine whenever he was in trouble, but now, when the horse came near, he folded his arms on the top of a fence and dropped his head upon them. He would not raise his face even when the stallion sniffed at his hair and whinnied in anxiety almost as faint as a human whisper.

28

THE truth came to him slowly as his head lay on his arms. Whatever hope of one day winning Sally had glimmered before him as the star haunts the pilot, was now vanished. He was roused to the dark reality of earthly facts: that Harry Chandler was the man she loved, and that without him she could never be happy. And if he loved her, all he could do was to bring her marriage to Chandler closer to realization. It would be like a pouring forth of blood, such a work. It would be more torment than all the long agony of the trail behind Moonshine, for that labor was undertaken in his own behalf, and this would be for another.

And to close the last door of hope and bolt it firmly shut is a grisly task. When Lee stood up straight again and turned away without a word or a touch for the waiting horse, he could feel the impress of pain, the wrinkles and the seams of new trouble, already stamped upon his face. He crossed the street and went straight toward the little shack which Chandler owned.

There was a light in the small house, but it was not the steady shining of a lamp. Instead, the spot of illumination jumped at random here and there, flashed across the window, or spilled through the open doorway and streaked the road with white. The light ceased to rove as Lee came close. It settled bright upon the face of a man in the hut, one who was packing down the burning coal of his pipe with a calloused forefinger before he answered. He was a great block of a man, with a mass of gray hair bristling on his head and whiskers masking the lower part of his face. He wore a red shirt, open at the throat, exposing a thick, corded, wrinkled neck. His fingers were habitually half bent, as though fixed in that position by many a year of polishing pick and shovel handle. He carried with him, also, that blunt and downright manner of those who tear their living out of the soil. And yet Lee Garrison, now drawn close, heard the voice of Sally McGuire address this stranger as her father.

"He's gone, Dad," said the girl. "I knew that would happen. You see everything is in confusion. He's taken his blankets. Harry's gone!"

"Let him stay," grunted McGuire. "A man that runs away after he's beaten isn't worth calling back."

"Father!" cried Sally.

"Sally!" mocked her father. His tone changed to a growl. "I'm tired of this temperamental stuff."

"Then I'll go myself!"

Lee Garrison listened with a hollow heart to the thrill and the sob in her voice.

"Go where?"

"To find poor Harry and bring him back and save him from despair. He'll do some desperate thing. He's capable of anything, now that he considers his life a failure."

"Rot," said McGuire. "He's off sulking. In a week he'll be back to marry you, if you're fool enough to throw yourself away on him."

"What possible right have you to speak of him like this? You know he'll never marry me unless he can support me. He's told you that himself."

"Which makes it Bible stuff, does it?"

"Now that he's down, you speak of him like this?"

"Never hit a man in my life when he was down. But I say,

195

give Harry rope, and he'll run in a circle and come back. He's like a small boy that's left home because he got a spanking. That's all."

"It's that detestable liar and hypocrite—" She could not finish the sentence. She paused indignant.

"You're blaming this on the gambler—on Garrison? I tell you, Sally, a fellow who can ride as he did today can't be all wrong. He gave you a promise to quiet you, that was all. Of course he couldn't keep it. And what under the heavens possessed you to try to buy him off!"

"To save Harry."

"A man that needs a woman's saving isn't worth being saved."

"I won't be answered with stale maxims. You talk as if I were a coward."

"There are more kinds of courage than that which takes a man through a fight."

Oh, wise, wise brain under that shock of wild gray hair, how the heart of Lee Garrison hung upon his words. It was as though a brave and skillful champion stood in the lists fighting his battle.

"You—you're like all the rest!" cried the girl. "You hate him because he failed today. But I tell you it only makes me prouder to fight for him and show him that my faith has never wavered."

"You don't have to tell me that. Give a woman a lost cause; that's all she wants. She'll throw her heart away on it! And you've found your hopeless case."

"Father!" cried Sally McGuire.

"Bah!" roared the inelegant McGuire. "That yap—that big fourflusher! He makes me tired. I saw through him a year ago. Man to man, Sally, like the honest little woman you are, confess to me that you are all wrapped up in

Chandler simply because you think you may be able to save him—make something useful out of him. Confess, Sally: It's a sort of missionary interest!"

She could master her indignation barely enough to permit speech. "Have you finished insulting me and the man I love?" she managed to ask.

"I'm through. But I couldn't hold in any longer. I've been swallowing what I think of Chandler all these months!"

"Then let me go out."

"Where?"

"To find him."

"Sally!"

"To find him if I have to spend the rest of my life in the search. Let me go, Dad!"

"Let you ride off alone—at night? Good heavens, Sally, are you mad?"

"I tell you I shall go!"

"Sally, this isn't like you. I've argued you into a frenzy. Don't ruin your life in following the first wild-headed impulse. By heavens, I'm talking to the wind! Sally, if you must go, I'll go with you!"

"I don't want you."

"You know that I'll never let you go alone. But, step out here and look at those black mountains. You see how foolish it is to try to follow him in this country?"

They passed through the doorway. They would surely have seen Lee Garrison as he shrank to the side had it not been that they were so filled with their own thoughts.

"I know where to find him," she declared, her voice made soft and smaller by the presence of the wide night. "When we came over the mountains, do you remember that gorge with a straight wall of rhyolite on one side and a slope tucked away under the bluff?"

"I remember," muttered McGuire. "It was just this side of The Captain."

"Yes, Harry and I both thought it was a lovely valley. And that day we agreed that—in a word, Dad, I know that Harry will go there first and wait to see if something doesn't bring me to him."

"He's mighty reckless," said McGuire. "He runs away without saying a word. Sally, it would take a night of riding. It would be dawn before we reached that valley under The Captain."

"Have I asked you to come?"

She hurried away, almost running, and Lee heard her father groan, then set out in pursuit. He watched them disappear. A fragment of talk from a passing group of men drifted upon his mind.

"I was sitting on a stull and gadding out a hitch. I heard the drum groaning out, and I knew that pair of mules had balked again. Pretty soon I hear Joe hollering down the shaft. He says to me: 'These here mules don't think much of this mine. They ain' got no heart in the work!' And I hollers back to Joe like I—"

The voice of the narrator drifted to an unintelligible jumble, and Garrison returned to his own thoughts. The talk he had overheard fitted into his preconceptions as perfectly as though it had been planned on a stage. Here was a demonstration which proved how utterly the girl loved Harry Chandler, how blank her life would be without him. All the doubts which had been lingering like hope in the corners of his brain were expelled.

He went back to the corral behind Mrs. Samuel's house. Moonshine greeted his return with an ecstasy, but Lee cut his antics short with the first abrupt word he had ever spoken to the stallion, and after that the horse stood quiet as a mouse, his head turned in wonder as he watched Lee saddle.

After that, Lee brought him to the front of the house. He carried out a hundred pounds of gold coin and dumped it into the saddlebags. Then he swung into the saddle and headed east and north toward The Captain.

29

DAWN found him in a wilderness of tumbled mountain heads, and while the rough crest of The Captain was bright with rosy light, Lee Garrison looked down beneath the great peak into a valley all awash with shadow. The south wall of that gulch was an abrupt cliff of rhyolite, a delicate mingling of colors, now, like a garden seen by the half lights of dusk. From the north there was a tumble of hills and smoothly dropping slopes, pine-covered, and where the trees crowded, thickened in the heart of the valley, a stream wound. He saw its silver flashing here and there.

The day grew momently brighter. The radiance stole down the rhyolite cliff to its base. The evergreens were shimmerings. In the clearings the narrow river flashed, and from one strip of white water he heard the deep and distant voice of the cascades. Morning had swept around him at a step. He moved to the left. Now he could see the base of the cliff, with a little cabin squatted against the rock in a setting of huge boulders; and a single horseman was going toward it. He needed no glass to spy that man out and tell he was Harry Chandler.

There was only one care in his mind when he sent the stallion down the slope in pursuit. He must be finished with Chandler and out of the valley before McGuire and Sally came up, and how far he was ahead of them he could not guess. For with that chinking burden in the saddlebags, he had spared Moonshine more than usual, more than there was need, it seemed, for now, at the end of that long, arduous trail, the gray ran as lightly as ever, his gallop as swift and free as the winging of a bird. Even on this grim morning that gallop raised the heart of Lee Garrison, made him lift his head, and brought the faintest of smiles upon his worn face.

He ran his hand with a caress along the neck of the horse, and Moonshine tossed his head with pricking ears and whinnied joyously as he ran. For, as Lee suddenly remembered, it was the first time during all the night that he had given the stallion so much as a touch of the hand, far less a single word to hearten him at his labor. And how happily Moonshine ran now, turning his head to examine the forest as he passed, or glancing up at an impudent hawk stooped close overhead, or bounding to the side with simulated fear as they shot past a lightning-stricken, white ghost of a tree.

The pines thinned before them, scattered to nothing, and curving around the shoulder of a low knoll, he came in view of Harry Chandler. He was in the act of drawing the saddle from a sweat-blackened horse, not a hundred yards away, at the door of the cabin.

And Harry saw him at the same instant. The saddle dropped from his hand. "What the devil do you mean by following?" he called.

"I'll tell you," answered Lee. His voice jerked away to nothing. A brook separated the two men, and Moonshine was crossing it as a greyhound could hardly have done, avoiding the cold black pools of deep water and leaping with consummate skill from the slippery rocks of one shallows to land with bunched feet on the next. So he wove his way across the stream with Lee enchanted by that adroitness until the yell of Chandler struck hammerlike against his ear over the rushing of the water.

"Keep back, Garrison. I warn you fairly; come a step nearer—"

What was in his mind? It was incredible; it was madness to think of—and yet now into Chandler's hand came the long, gleaming body of a Colt revolver.

"Keep back!" he yelled. And before Lee could rally his bewildered wits, before he could swerve the gray horse with a touch on the bridle: "Then take it on your own head, damn you!"

The gun barked, jerking up its nose with the recoil as though rearing to see what mischief it had done. Mischief enough! For Moonshine stopped and half reared as the bullet struck, then rallied and sprang for the shore. As for Lee, he could not move, he could not think. This was a dream of things which could not be. Only in a nightmare could a man stand with black hatred in his face and murder a horse! But there was Harry Chandler, transformed to a fiend, bringing down his revolver to the level again.

Once more! The report broke louder as they left the voice of the creek. Moonshine twisted in mid-air. He struck the bank with a force that knocked Lee from the saddle, and sent him spinning over and over in the dirt and gravel, till a log stopped him with a crash. He saw Moonshine turning toward him and sinking on trembling legs. Down slumped the hind quarters. Still, propped on the shaking forelegs, his ears pricked, the gray horse neighed toward the master and struggled in vain to lift himself and come. But all that unmatchable strength was withering out of his body. There was no power of sinew and muscle now, but still the great spirit looked out of his eyes at Lee, and there was never a glance for the man who was killing him. One knee buckled to the ground, then the other, the proud neck with its wind-lifted mane fell lower, and Moonshine lay dead among the rocks.

"And now you!" shouted the madman who had been Harry Chandler.

He shattered the stream of his own oaths with the explosions of his gun. A handful of gravel was scuffed into the face of Lee Garrison. That was the work of the first bullet. The second spattered to water on the face of a quartzite rock. Then Lee came to his feet. That he was facing a leveled revolver did not matter. That the man behind the gun bulked twice as large as he, was a little thing. A sort of insane energy was burning in his brain, turning his muscles to iron. To the hysterical speed with which his mind was working the movements of Harry seemed ridiculously slow, as though he were gesturing on a stage. His revolver had jammed as Lee sprang up. He struggled with it an instant, then hurled it at the head of Garrison. It brushed past the ear of Lee, and the next instant Lee had closed on the murderer, his stiff fingers buried in flesh.

It was strangely easy. He was filled with perfect certainty, complete assurance. The fist of Harry beat into his face. He caught that flying arm by the wrist. He held it with bone-crushing force, and smiled into the eyes of Harry. Chandler shrieked as even a brave man cries out when a beast closes on him. He strove to tear himself free, but his powerful body was turned to a figure of sand. Lee Garrison raised him as he might have lifted a great loosely filled sack and dashed him to the ground. The head of Harry struck a rock, jarred far to the side, and then the great body lay still.

Lee went back to the horse, but the brave eyes were dull. He ran his fingers down the neck, silken smooth, still warm with life. Realization came to him in wave on wave as a ship sinks, staggering down, down, till the water licks quite across its decks. Moonshine would never rise again. Moonshine would never run again. Moonshine was dead!

So the fruit of that first great adventure was vanished. Then he turned to Chandler with the last of his insane fury melting out of his brain. The strength left his body. His limbs trembled, and his knees shook under his weight as he went to see if the quest were indeed ended with two deaths.

Crimson stained the pebbles on which the head of Chandler lay. His eyes were closed, his face wax-pale, but even as Lee dropped to his knees beside him the prostrate man stirred, groaned, opened his eyes. The nightmare of fear came back into them as he saw Lee. He dared not rise.

"Sit up," said Lee.

The other obeyed.

"Stand up."

Chandler rose.

"You're not hurt bad," said Lee. "Go inside the cabin. There's something out here we don't want to see."

Chandler cast a glance at the body of the stallion, another wild glance at Lee, still a third look at the revolver he had thrown away, and obeyed. As for Lee, he delayed only to unbuckle the saddlebags. Then he followed in and cast the pouches of coin upon the floor; they fell with a heavy crunching of metal.

Harry had tied a white handkerchief around his head to stop the bleeding. Now he sat on the side of a bunk which was built against the wall in one corner of the shack.

"Chandler," said Lee, "you shot to kill Moonshine."

The fascinated eyes of Chandler widened, fixed on the revolver which hung in the other's holster, then jerked up to his face.

"I shot for you, Garrison," he said. "That first time I aimed to get you, and when I saw that I'd missed and hit the horse instead—I went crazy—I didn't know what I was doing."

"So you shot again—at Moonshine."

Chandler drew in a long, gasping breath. He was collapsing, shrinking smaller and smaller.

"I didn't know what I was doing, I—" His voice was beginning to tremble, sure warning that he was about to break down, and a horror came to Lee of the shameful thing which might be just ahead.

"I believe you, Harry," he said hurriedly. "I've got to believe you. I believe that you aimed to get me with that first slug, and—otherwise, what sort of a husband would you make for her? How could she be happy with you?"

The question broke off sharply.

He was talking swiftly, arguing with himself, and such arguments are always won.

"Chandler, I've heard about you. You've told Sally you'll not marry her till you've got money of your own to support her. Maybe you'd like to change your mind. Maybe it's fear of her father that keeps you from changing. I dunno, but I guess a lot. Only the main thing is that she wants you. Look here, Chandler. Here's more'n ten thousand dollars in cash. That's stake enough for a man to marry on. It's money that Moonshine made for me, and I'll never use it."

"Just a moment," said Harry. He started up from his seat. "Did you trail me up here to offer me that?"

"Yes."

"And I—what have I done to you? Garrison, can you forgive me?"

The hand which he had extended fell.

"If it had been me that dropped," said Lee, "and if I'd

seen Moonshine running free while I died, then I could of forgiven you clean and free. It would have been the right ending. Now what matters is that she wants you. Will you go to her?"

"Man, man," said Harry, "how can I take your money?"

"Because all I can do for her is to give her the man she loves. You'll take what I offer? You'll swear to go back to her?"

His voice had risen, and Chandler shrank back from him.

"I swear, Garrison."

"Saddle your hoss and start. Ride down the valley. You'll meet her coming this way."

He sat on the edge of the bunk with his face dropped in his hands. He heard the floor creak under the weight of Chandler; heard the rattle of the coin as the saddlebags were lifted; heard the flop of the saddle as it was swung onto the back of the horse. He heard the creak and strain of the stirrup leather as Chandler lifted himself into place. He heard the grinding of pebbles under hoof. And still he waited through the dragging moments. At last he went out. He sat down by his horse and took the lifeless head in his lap.

Now into his mind flowed the quiet music of the creek, and beyond that the bird voices out of the trees or in the wind; and he heard, too, the buzz and faint singing of insects hunting through the grass around him. But above all these noises the silence of the mountains was king, just as it overpowered the tumult of the mines in Crooked Creek. And he knew that when the years went by him the happy days to which his mind would go back were those times when, in the long agony of the quest for Moonshine, he had paused in the morning or the twilight and waited for the mountain silence to step in swiftly around him, and in his memory and in his daydreams, Moonshine would never be captured!

A shadow fell across the brightness of his spur, and he looked up into the face of Sally McGuire standing beside him! Had she dropped out of the bodiless air? There, behind her, seated on a boulder near the cabin sat McGuire himself, scowling down at the ground and puffing steadily at his pipe. How long ago could they have come up the trail under the cliff?

But miracles were happening. Sally dropped to her knees. Her hands were clasped in her lap, and great tears were dropping one by one. He looked up from her hands to her face in awe, and her wide, tear-saddened eyes looked into his for a moment.

"Oh, Lee," she said, "we'll raise a monument for him, and we'll carve his name—"

She bowed her face into her hands and sobbed.

"But," said McGuire on a day not very long after this, "was it really the cabin we lived in that summer in the Samson Mountains?"

"Of course not," said Sally, "and I never had such a glove as that in my life. But I'll never be able to tell Lee, poor dear."

OLD MASTER OF
THE OLD WEST
MAX BRAND

**Thundering action that never quits—Max Brand
lets you have it just the way you want it.
For the very best in Western entertainment, get
these Max Brand titles, available from
Pocket Books:**

_____	82890	BELLS OF SAN FILIPO $1.75
_____	82893	DANGER TRAIL $1.75
_____	82887	FIGHTING FOUR $1.75
_____	82894	HUNTED RIDERS $1.75
_____	82888	LONGHORN FEUD $1.75
_____	82885	LONG, LONG TRAIL $1.75
_____	82891	OUTLAW OF BUFFALO FLAT $1.75
_____	82886	RAWHIDE JUSTICE $1.75
_____	82892	REWARD $1.75
_____	82889	SEVEN TRAILS $1.75
_____	81751	SHOTGUN LAW $1.75
_____	83416	THE OUTLAW $1.75

WESTERNS
THAT NEVER DIE

They pack excitement that lasts a lifetime.
It's no wonder Zane Grey is the bestselling
Western writer of all time.
Get these Zane Grey Western adventures
from Pocket Books:

_____ 83102 BORDER LEGION $1.75

_____ 82896 BOULDER DAM $1.75

_____ 83422 RIDERS OF THE PURPLE SAGE $1.95

_____ 82692 DEER STALKER $1.75

_____ 82883 KNIGHTS OF THE RANGE $1.75

_____ 82878 ROBBERS ROOST $1.75

_____ 82076 TO THE LAST MAN $1.75

_____ 83534 UNDER THE TONTO RIM $1.95

_____ 82880 U.P. TRAIL $1.75

_____ 83022 ARIZONA CLAN $1.75

_____ 83105 BLACK MESA $1.75

_____ 83309 CALL OF THE CANYON $1.75

36